Money Matters

A Novel

Brian Finney

contact@bhfinney.com

www.bhfinney.com

ISBN-13: 978-0-9998003-1-7

For Jacky

Wealth is the ability to truly experience life.

—Henry David Thoreau

ACKNOWLEDGMENTS

Thanks to David P. for the brilliant notes, to Meredith M. for the amazingly detailed, professional editing, to Paul Tidwell for a meticulous copy edit, to all those who contributed reviews, to Carl Graves at Extended Imagery for the beautiful book design, and especially to Nanda Dyssou and Coriolis Company for helping me launch this novel into today's digital environment with such talent and expertise.

TABLE OF CONTENTS

FRIDAY,

OCTOBER 29, 2010

D ammit! What's your problem, I curse at myself in the mirror, applying my morning lipstick. What the hell are you doing living in your sister Tricia's ultramodern soulless Venice condo (or New York–style live/work loft, as realtors like my sister call it)? You're twenty-seven, and you still don't even have a place of your own.

As I brush my long brown hair that cries out for a stylist's scissors, I recall what made me move in here two years ago. I was renting a small studio apartment in an undistinguished Mar Vista apartment building, the rent made manageable by its location one block from noisy Venice Boulevard. The owner lived on the ground floor. She was a born-again Christian, and she made sure everyone knew it. One evening I had a surprise visit from Juan, a fellow ex-student at Santa Monica College. We hadn't seen each other since we graduated, and he had moved east. He was a handsome guy whose parents had brought him from Mexico as a baby. He had a black drooping mustache and long matching hair. He was gay and very popular at school. We had become friends in our junior year and done lots of fun things together.

He was only in town for twenty-four hours, and that evening we consumed a pizza and two bottles of wine between us. At the end of the evening he decided that he had had too much alcohol to drive his rental car back to his hotel. So I offered him my bed and slept on the sofa, which was too small for him. Early the following morning we were awakened by a continuous ringing of the doorbell. Slipping a coat over my nightshirt I opened the door to find the enraged building owner eying me and Juan, who was looking up sleepily from my bed.

"Miss Carter, I told you when I rented you this studio that I did not allow any illegal activities." Indignation made her puce in the face.

"What are you talking about?" I was genuinely confused.

"I won't stand for any immorality in my place. You can't bring johns here. No way."

"*Johns?* What are you talking about? What makes you think Juan here is a john?"

"It's obvious. He's Mexican."

"And what's that got to do with anything?" I was beginning to get as heated as she was.

"You're white, aren't you?"

"So?"

"Well, he's not. Must be a paying client."

"He's a friend, for Christ's sake."

"Don't you take the name of the Lord in vain. A friend! Very likely!"

"You don't know what you're talking about. Besides, he's gay."

At this remark she turned apoplectic. "That does it. I don't tolerate perverts. You've got till the end of the month to clear out."

"Are you serious?"

"You bet I'm serious. You better be out by the thirty-first, or your belongings will be out on the sidewalk."

"What a pitiful bigot you are," I shouted, and slammed the door in her face.

I had only ten days to find a place I could afford, and there was nothing on the West Side available at that price. So I put my pride aside and asked Tricia if I could temporarily move into her place.

"You can have the spare bedroom and bathroom for $1,200 a month," she answered.

Money always did come first with her. I see money as a means, not an end. But a means to what? Self-fulfillment? Independence—especially from Tricia? I've never had to answer that question, because I've barely gotten by with poorly paid, part-time jobs.

Tricia and I share the kitchen and living room—with difficulty. Our problem isn't just traditional sibling rivalry, although there's been plenty of that. We're such diametric opposites that we disagree about almost everything—down to how to tie shoelaces or mix a drink. She's all wham-bam, make it happen the way you want it to. She just can't stand my more deliberate approach—what she calls my passivity.

It's been this way for as long as I can remember. Although my sister is barely two years older than me, she's always treated me like a naive child. From the start she acted as my protector, which just made her madder about my supposed inexperience.

One afternoon when I was four, she'd just come home from school. I was playing with a new toy phone. I loved it; each of the brightly colored keypad numbers played a different tune when I pressed it. I was entranced by it. Tricia asked me where I got it. I told her I'd used my birthday money to buy it.

"How much did it cost?"

"Seven-fifty."

"What a stupid waste of money," she snorted.

"Why?" I asked indignantly.

"Because you could have asked to play with either Mom's or Dad's real phones. Much more interesting, and they cost nothing."

"But I wanted my own phone," I said.

"And how long will ten different rings keep you happy?"

I stopped playing with that toy the same day and never picked it up again.

I look at my face in the mirror, now, for the millionth time. After twenty-seven years it still lacks firm definition. My dark brown eyes seem to be perpetually asking an unanswerable question. My small, straight nose and rosy cheeks give me the look of a country girl. Yet people tell me I'm attractive, and I get enough come-ons from men to believe it. I know I'm only talking about externals here. But in Los Angeles externals are everything. And my externals tell me that I'm an equivocator. An accommodator. Too much deference, too little pushback. Too much consideration for everyone else, too little for myself.

I don't know why, but I feel that I'm approaching a turning point in my life. I feel so much pressure within me that I might explode at any moment. I simply cannot go on as I am.

What is it with me? If I could answer that, I wouldn't be in this state of confusion. I have zero confidence in myself. I no longer feel that I have made the right life choices and that Tricia's are wrong. After all, who's living in whose apartment? Still, I have no wish to emulate her. I find her lifestyle and ideas utterly alien.

I feel I need to change everything about my life. I wish something external would force me to do that. Living with Tricia for two years has undermined my self-confidence, leaving me dissatisfied with who I am now but unmotivated to change it. What's keeping me from taking charge of my life?

*

In the kitchen, I find Tricia ready to meet her first clients of the day, ready to try to sell them an overpriced, 1920s Venice bungalow—"a teardown," she calls it—that has been way too long on the market. Tricia won't tell her clients about the hoops they'll have to jump through to get the City Planning Department and the California Coastal Commission to let them demolish the house. Of course she won't: her commission on the sale will be at least $50,000—more than I earn in a year.

"Morning, Jenny," she greets me, barely looking round from her Italian espresso machine. "You look a mess."

Tricia sees herself as a smart businesswoman, which she is, and dresses to fit the part. This morning she's wearing a dark gray Roberto Cavalli wool business suit with a low neckline that offers male buyers an added incentive to clinch the deal. Sex, Tricia says, is a business tool. She's always asking me why I'm wasting my sexual assets on "Dreary" (her pointedly unaffectionate nickname for my boyfriend Gary). And, I have to say, she can be super-sexy. Her male clients have difficulty keeping their eyes focused on her face. Strangely, she herself is only attracted to the brasher and equally self-confident bachelors who play the LA singles field with as much expertise as she does. Maybe she enjoys the challenge. She's a born fighter.

An inch taller and two years older than I am, Tricia sees her appearance as her most important investment, and she spends accordingly. Her $600 Beverly Hills stylist cuts her hair at a merciless angle. Her brown eyes appear blue thanks to tinted contact lenses. Her aesthetician threads her eyebrows weekly. Of course, she wears false lashes (one hundred percent human hair, individually hand placed) enhanced by Clé de Peau Beauté mascara. Her small, upturned nose, which used to look exactly like mine, is the work of LA's premier cosmetic surgeon. Her lips are collagen-enhanced, embellished by her signature Yves Saint Laurent Rouge Vernis lipstick.

Tricia cannot seem to keep herself from offering me advice. "Get real," she's been telling me for years. "Money matters. Stop doing plant maintenance for that client of yours and open your own plant store. Stop working part-time for Total Surveillance and start your own detective agency. Better yet, get your plant client who owns Wealth Management to give you a job, so that you can finally earn some serious money."

She's talking about Todd Granger. His company, Balboa Wealth Management Corporation, is the second-biggest mutual fund corporation in the country. I'm sure he could get me into his world—if I wanted him to, that is. But do I want him to do that? What do I want?

What do I really want?

Sure, money matters. But so does what you have to do to make it. Tricia's at the mercy of her smartphone day and night. Her clients make sure she earns her commission by making her life as miserable as they can manage. They're constantly changing their minds, asking for more, more, more, all while trying to bargain down her commission. In turn, Tricia despises them and trashes them behind their backs. If that's what it takes to earn serious money, I don't want it.

"I know you meant to put the coffee grinder back into the cabinet yesterday instead of leaving it on the counter." This is Tricia's opening shot of the morning. Instantly I'm transformed in her eyes—and my own—to the recalcitrant child who forgets to put her toys away.

Tricia sees her superior income as a confirmation of my immaturity. This, in turn, justifies her taking on the role of a strict, irritating parent, a role neither of us enjoys, but we cannot seem to escape it. I can hear her thoughts. Why can't you understand the way this country works? When are you going to grow up? When are you going to learn not to put out unless the return on your investment makes it worthwhile?

Tricia fills her hideous portable traveling mug (reflective puce with soft rubbery handle) with coffee and drops it into her burgundy Italian leather purse, which she deftly slings over her shoulder.

"Your turn to sift Lulu's litter," she says with a sigh. "I wish I didn't have to remind you every time."

Needless to say, Tricia and I have different ideas of how often the cat box needs attention. Tricia always has been anal. Plus she hates the fact that Lulu, her long-haired black-and-white cat, prefers to sleep with me, which she does whenever Tricia can't find her at night to lock her in her own bedroom. Lulu's one of those rare cats who loves to sleep snuggling against a warm body. Some summer nights I wake up running with sweat because Lulu is generating double body heat. Tricia can't stand that much closeness. But she wants Lulu to acknowledge that Lulu belongs to her, not to me.

*

I remember one night in our early childhood when Tricia and I were still sharing a bedroom—I must have been about five and she seven. I always slept with my teddy bear, Cuddles, pressed to my chest. I had a habit of talking to Cuddles and then answering myself in "his" voice, and that night Tricia lost her cool and snatched Cuddles away from me.

"Why are you talking to a stuffed piece of fabric with plastic beads for eyes?" she spat at me.

"Why," I had Cuddles ask me, "does your sister have no imagination?"

"And stop pretending that it's Cuddles who's talking."

Cuddles responded, "You're not the only one who can talk."

"Stop it!" she screamed. "Or I'll throw Cuddles out the window."

"If you throw me out of the window," Cuddles replied smugly, "Jenny will cry her head off, and your parents will run in here and give you a hard time."

"Just grow up, can't you?" Tricia threw Cuddles at me. That was one of the rare fights in which I (or at least Cuddles) held our own.

Tricia always has been better than I am at dealing with the world. She sees me as hopelessly passive and out of touch with her world of big money and competition, the only thing that makes her feel truly alive. But I see the other side to her triumphs. The high she gets from winning a fight dissipates the minute she's won, leaving her longing for the next challenge. Plus her inevitable defeats bring on lows that last until her next win.

I don't want the lows, but I worry sometimes that I never experience highs like her. Is my life too bland? Am I afraid of taking risks? Am I too dependent on my sister? My boyfriend? My employers?

Tricia is my alter ego: what I resist, and what I need. I refuse to believe that the measure of everything in life is what you pay for it. How do you put a price on happy memories? Or regrets? Or longings that spur you on to your next move? Why, then, do I spend so much of my time worrying about the money I don't have? Maybe because I can't afford to fix the brakes on my car, which urgently need fixing.

*

My reverie is interrupted by my iPhone's ringtone, the chorus from Madonna's "Like A Virgin," my favorite song as a teen. I hit "Accept" and hear the voice of Felicia, Todd Granger's housekeeper, who takes care of his enormous mansion in Newport Beach. Twice a week I tend to his houseplants. I don't know what Todd pays Felicia, but I get $15 an hour. That's not bad for the floral industry.

Felicia and I have bonded, as coworkers first, then as friends, despite our very different backgrounds. Felicia came to LA from Oaxaca in her late teens. She's like a good mother to me, the only person who believes in me completely. Which leaves me feeling guilty, since I don't deserve that kind of faith.

"I so worried." Felicia's grammar goes especially to pieces when she gets emotional. "Susan disappeared."

Susan Kirby was Todd's live-in girlfriend for two years until she ditched him three months ago. Felicia adored Susan, who treated her as an equal. Felicia was shocked when Susan and Todd broke up.

"What do you mean 'missing'?" I ask.

"I tried to call and call. Finally, I went to her apartment in Palos Verdes, and it was no right. I could see through the window. All the plants were muertas. Plates broken on the kitchen floor."

"She must have moved," I say.

"No! No! The landlord told me she pays the rent. Is not right. Something is malo. It smell bad in there."

"What does the landlord say?"

"He not care if he gets his dinero. What do I do?"

"She's probably gone away somewhere to get over Todd."

"No. She called me every weekend until she leave the house of Señor Granger. She is a friend. Then nothing. I try to call almost every day. Last week it say her machine full. I know something is wrong. Estoy preocupada. You are detective. You can find someone." As I said, she believes in me, which is more than I do.

"Hardly a detective. I just review videotapes for a big detective agency."

"You are modest."

"Just telling the truth."

"You're the only detective I know."

"Okay," I say, cursing myself for agreeing. "I'll look into it."

Here I go again, I reflect. Volunteering for more unpaid work. And it's work I'm not even qualified to undertake. But at least it's for someone I care about. I can imagine Tricia laughing her head off at me: "Why can't you learn to say the simple word 'No'?"

"Thank you so much, amiga. Adiós."

"Adiós, Felicia."

What's done is done. Coffee, a slice of toast, then the 405 to Newport Beach. At least I remember to put the coffee grinder away.

*

I drive south through the parking lot that doubles as the 405 freeway, thinking about Susan Kirby. Tall, slim, short-cut blond hair, in her thirties, Susan dressed conservatively by day in pressed slacks, tailored blouses, and minimal makeup. She didn't need much help in the looks department, with her wide grey-blue eyes, sensuous lips, and enviable figure. Susan was gifted as a personality, too, with a wonderful sense of humor and an interest in everything and everyone in her radius, including Felicia and me.

Felicia worshipped Susan. Susan genuinely seemed to think of Felicia as a friend. It was always left for Todd to issue any orders on the rare occasions they were needed. Felicia is one of those exceptional workers who anticipate their employers' needs most of the time. Susan called Felicia Lici and insisted that Felicia call her Susan, not Miss Kirby.

I catch myself thinking about Susan in the past tense and tell myself to stop being morbid.

I remember the morning when Todd joined Felicia and me in the kitchen and told us that he and Susan had had a "falling out." "I'm sorry to tell you that Susan is no longer living here."

Felicia looked shocked. "But why, Señor Granger?"

"She no longer wants to live here."

This was hardly an explanation, but neither Felicia nor I was in any position to press for details.

"I will miss her."

"I will, too," Todd said with what seemed like genuine sadness.

Felicia was devastated by Susan's departure. For the rest of that day she kept bursting into tears. "Why Señor Granger not try to talk with Susan? He's a good man. He will miss her muchisimo." But it's clear that it's Felicia who misses Susan, not Todd, who rarely mentions her name. Of course, that could be a way of hiding his hurt from us. Or from himself.

Susan would never let Felicia do anything personal for her, like make her a cup of coffee or take her clothes to the cleaner. "You're employed by Todd," Susan would tell Felicia, "not me." Felicia cooked their dinners most weeknights, and Todd chose the menu. Susan often joined Felicia to do the Thursday shopping at the Costa Mesa farmers market. Felicia told me that Susan knew many of the sellers by name ("Hi, Dave," she'd call out. "I want some of your ripest dragon fruit." "For you, darling, nothing but the best.") She and Felicia would have lunch under the umbrella-covered tables there, usually, according to Felicia, favoring the sushi food truck (Susan had the appetite of a bird). And she'd carry half the purchases herself back to the car. She sure humanized the household.

As I drive south I'm wondering what made her leave Todd? What happened between them that made her return to the job market when she'd seemed so happy living a life of leisure and fulfillment? Todd made it sound like the breakup was Susan's choice. But I've learned never to trust either member of a couple to truthfully explain their breakup. The past always gets reshaped to suit the present.

Do I see Susan as my model self? A woman who seemed to derive complete satisfaction from living on her own terms without getting caught up in the whirl of money and possessions? Do I see her as my better self? Am I looking as much for my missing self as I am for her? If she is as admirable as I believe, was her breakup with Todd a sign that the man she obviously cared for had crossed some kind of line of hers? Because Susan was no compromiser. She knew what she wanted from life and would not hesitate to split from someone who didn't live up to her expectations. What might Todd have done to drive her away?

*

The car radio is playing Rihanna's "Love the Way You Lie." I remember the video of the fight the two get into (he's singing, "You push, pull each other's hair, scratch, claw . . ."). He's abusive. He's also a very emotional being, which is why he hits her and then swears he'll never do it again ("though I know it's lies"). How unlike Gary and me. I can't imagine him ever losing his cool. King of bland. But what about my part in it? That's probably why we've been together as long as we have.

Come to think of it, my parents had a pretty bland relationship. There were none of the fireworks that sometimes erupted in the homes of my high school friends. If my parents disagreed about something Dad would call time out, they'd sit down at the kitchen table, and each would give the other five uninterrupted minutes in which to argue his or her side. I saw them almost contorting themselves to reach a compromise. God forbid that they should end up with opposing opinions. That would have been too threatening for them. I try to imagine what would have happened if one of them had lost it and gone off the deep end. It might have been a lot healthier. But they seemed to think that a truly angry outburst would set them on the primrose path to divorce.

Maybe Tricia got her aggression in opposition to them. Somehow she managed to cultivate the art of listening to her own feelings and acting on them. Selfish? Maybe. But decisive. A woman who seems to have no doubts. I, on the other hand, took from my parents a compulsion to doubt authorities and authoritarian stances of all kinds.

Still, at the time I admired my parents' determination to work things out in a civilized way. I admired their keen social conscience, their insistence on thinking beyond their own needs and desires. But now I see them as stranded by the flash flood of life, bewildered by the fast-moving waters of my digital generation sweeping past them. They've never criticized Tricia in front of me, but I wonder what they really think about some of her values. Most likely they find some way of rationalizing away whatever she throws at them.

Mom was always very anti-war. She condemned even America's repulse of Hussein's invasion of Kuwait in the Gulf War. She blamed the Pentagon's inflated budget for America's failure to take care of its poor and disadvantaged. Her bumper sticker read PEACE POWER— a perfect image of her confusion, seeing that peace involves renouncing power. Mom and Dad met on a peace march. Together they got petitions signed, organized bake sales, and the like. They believed that they could curb the power of the corporations and the Pentagon.

I inherited their liberal outlook, but not their belief in acts of resistance. Recently Dad said to me, "Look at how Obama got himself elected with millions of small contributions. We can change everything if enough Americans believe we can." But look at what happened after 2008. Party warfare. Washington gridlock. Accusations of socialism (a current term of abuse), of appointing death panels for the elderly— the list goes on. And now everyone is forecasting a landslide for the Republicans this coming Tuesday. Dad: "Pollsters are always wrong. You wait and see. I put my bet on Americans' common sense." I'm waiting. But I don't share his optimism, even while I wish I had his sense of commitment.

Work calls.

I arrive at the Granger mansion, all 8,000 square feet of it, perched at the end of Bay Island's natural promontory, surrounded on three sides by the sea. At night the glimmering lights from the houses on the mainland add to the illusion that the mansion is floating on the water.

The estate includes Todd's own private beach and dock, a swimming pool surrounded by cushy lounge chairs, and endless rolling lawns with deck chairs and barbecue pits. When he invited me to his Halloween party I got to see the place at night, the patios lined with long firepits that lit up the seawater lapping at his white sandy beach.

It takes me about five hours to take care of Todd's indoor plants. Most of the containers they're in are precious and fragile. In the bedroom, for example, there are two large Italian amphoras colored with a turquoise-and-terracotta drip glaze, that contain purple phalaenopsis orchids. In the entrance hall a porcelain Chinese fishbowl on a rosewood stand holds a scented Arabian jasmine with its clusters of white double flowers that turn green at the center. Although Todd says it's not necessary, I'm nervous enough about water spills to insist on moving the containers to a sink or a tarp when I water the plants or change them. So everything takes longer than it should. Todd pays me for twice-weekly visits. Monday I take care of the plants on the upper two floors. Fridays are for the ground floor.

When Todd or his brother Dan is at home I feel compelled to spend (unpaid) time chatting with them. I like Todd, though I don't worship him the way Felicia does—and no wonder, he's been very good to her. He gives her generous year-end bonuses—she confided to me that he gave her $2,000 last year, significantly more than ever before. He even bought her a secondhand car several years ago, and he helped get her son into Balboa Target School. Felicia is fiercely independent, so she never mentions her financial problems in front of Todd. But he knows, and he never fails to help her out.

Once all the plants on the rest of the ground floor are trimmed and watered, I knock on Todd's office door. He calls to me to come in. I find him sitting at his desk, and I think, as I often do when I see him, what a handsome man he is, especially for a guy in his early fifties. He could be a model or an actor. He wears his full, slightly graying hair swept back, accentuating his piercing gray eyes, tanned face, and perfectly shaped white teeth. He mostly wears Dolce & Gabbana suits over a white shirt with contrasting patterned cuffs and collar. His upright posture and relaxed smile exude confidence and success.

"Hi, Todd," I greet him. I gesture at a huge plant in the corner. "I'm going to swap that red ginger for something different I brought you today."

"Susan gave me that for my birthday last year. You're not thinking of dumping it, are you?"

I'm surprised at his bringing up her name, something he has avoided for the past three months.

"I know. I helped her choose it for you," I reply. "I'll keep it for you until next year when it's ready to bloom again."

"I'd appreciate that."

I screw up my courage to ask him the next question, the one I promised Felicia I'd ask.

"Felicia told me that she hasn't heard from Susan since she left. She and Felicia normally talked to one another weekends. Have you by any chance heard from her?"

Todd looks uncomfortable. I feel as if I'm treading all over his feelings. This detective work doesn't come easily.

"Not a word." Now he won't look me in the eye. I feel bad. But the investigative me has a nagging doubt—is he telling the truth? A professional detective would push this further. But I care too much about Todd's feelings to do so. Stuck in the middle again.

Todd's brother Dan walks in. I don't like him. He's smarmy in his regulation dark blue suits and red tie. Actually I find him downright creepy, and, when we're alone, he makes verbal passes at me that he disguises with stupid jokes. "Would you step away from the freezer? You're melting the ice cubes."

Dan is married and cares too much about his political career to risk an extramarital scandal, which makes his verbal come-ons all the creepier. I also hate his politics. He's a Republican state senator, running for governor. Like most politicians, he stands for whatever he thinks will make voters like him. The main plank of his platform is to get tough on illegal immigrants. As Felicia tells me, this puts every immigrant, legal and illegal, into the crosshairs, because it subjects the entire Mexican American community to more frequent searches and arrests for no good reason.

This is more than politics for Felicia. Her undocumented cousin, Miguel, works at Cal Fowl, an Azusa poultry processing plant. When Felicia told me how they kill the chickens I thought, that's a job that only an illegal immigrant would be willing to do. He would have to enter a half-life of evasion and fear should Dan get elected.

"Hi, Todd," Dan says, and to me: "How is our garden rose today?" I want to punch him. He's appropriating a term of endearment that only Todd uses for me.

"Enjoying my day in the sun," I reply. I move to the ginger, spread a tarp on the floor for it, and start to ease it out of its container.

Dan turns to Todd. "I need to talk to you about the campaign. Jill tells me we need to start paying some of those overdue bills."

"I told you not to worry about it," Todd says. "I'll have Bob write a check."

"What would we do without the Supreme Court," Dan quips.

"Or the Founding Fathers," Todd rejoins grinning.

I have a vague idea of what they're talking about. It has to do with a Supreme Court decision made last January that allows corporations to contribute huge sums to political campaigns in the name of free speech. To me the idea that corporations have voices, as if they're actual humans, seems totally weird. But what do I know? My main source of news is NPR when I'm in the car. Admittedly that seems like half my life, but still, my information comes in arbitrary snatches of stories that I catch partway through as I turn on the car and are cut short when I get wherever I'm going.

Todd turns to me. "I'd really like to have a new purple cattleya orchid for my desk. You're going to scold me for throwing my money away, aren't you?"

"I only do that when you want to replace perfectly good dormant plants with new ones. Sure, I'll get you a cattleya."

Todd explains to Dan: "Jenny takes my plants home and nurses them as if they were my kids."

"Maybe she'll give you that treatment someday," Dan responds.

Todd ignores his brother's crude insinuation.

Having finished replacing the plant, I excuse myself and leave them to their business and make for the kitchen to pass on to Felicia the outcome of my questions to Todd.

*

On my way to my car I pause in the driveway to check my social streams. Social media makes me especially schizophrenic. It's full of posturing, narcissism, and insecurity. At the same time, it's my generation's medium. I often ridicule what I read there. But that doesn't stop me from using it. My problem is not so much with the medium itself, as with the temptation it offers, its invitation to its users to expose themselves to the world, to become dependent on the "likes" of others. That leaves me torn between ridicule and pity. With social media, as with too many things, I seem unable to make up my mind exactly how I feel about it.

Here's Amy, my college roommate, now dating a software wiz, on Twitter: "omg. im done with texting today" (who cares? I bet she's not done). My fourteen-year-old cousin June tweets: "I don't want guys to put me on a petal stool." (I guess that's how we all add to our vocabulary by repeating phrases we've overheard.) I switch to Instagram. Scrolling down I come across a selfie taken by Amy. A headshot. It's clear to anyone who knows her that she has manipulated (or more likely had manipulated for her) her image: the mole on her chin has been removed, her eyelashes darkened, the color of her pupils altered from gray to blue, her cheekbones highlighted, and her teeth whitened as if she's starring in a toothpaste commercial. She's added a hashtag: "#hotnightwithmyBESTguy." I don't get it. Who's she trying to kid? I turn off my iPhone and get in my car. Time to grab a salad at Taco Bell and then head north.

*

On Friday afternoons the 405 going north, like every other frigging freeway in the area, slows to a maddening series of stops and starts. Most of the male drivers around me look too tired to inspire my sexual fantasies. Or am I the one who's too tired? On the car radio KCSN is in the middle of "No Line on the Horizon" by U2. That wakes me up instantly. ("I know a girl, a hole in her heart . . ." That's me). I'm headed for the Century City headquarters of Total Surveillance, LA's largest (and most expensive) private investigative agency. There I will spend four tedious and instantly forgettable hours in a cubicle fast-forwarding through surveillance tapes looking for evidence that only occasionally shows up. For $12 an hour! What is it with me? $48 minus deductions for giving up my evening. Why am I still just getting by doing such menial work? What is wrong with earning good money?

Why do I subconsciously distrust the whole world of money? Earning the derisory amount of it I do only facilitates the accumulation of wealth by the one or five percent.

After Total Surveillance comes another stimulating late evening with Gary of no fixed address, who bums off his friends, including me. Gary spends all his time playing military video games. Nothing, including me, seems to turn him on more than a new video game. One of the few ways of distracting him is unfastening his pants. What's wrong with him? He should be wanting to unfasten mine. No, wait. What's the matter with me? I should be dropping him, not his pants. Instead I keep on making up to this couch potato as if he were God, or next best, George Clooney.

As if by Pavlovian instinct, I turn on KCRW at the top of the hour, just in time for the news. At a rally in Burbank, GOP gubernatorial nominee Dan Granger predicted victory: "This is a very important election. It is the battle for the soul of California." I ask myself, what the hell does Dan mean by the soul of California? What does he know about souls, seeing that he appears to lack one of his own? He talks about erecting an economic barrier to keep employers from hiring illegal aliens, as if Mexicans were invaders from outer space.

The tall tower of Total Surveillance fills my windshield. Its blank reflective facade predicts the blank experience of the hours, weeks, years I'll be spending inside it. I pull into the underground parking lot with its low-level lighting, unnerving absence of humans, and hot stale air. I make for the stairway to give myself what exercise I can.

I settle into one of eight identical cubicles in the near-empty office, position my iPod headphones over my ears, and select Taylor Swift's *Speak Now*. Then I get to work reviewing security tapes. My first video in the pile left for me is marked RAUL PEREZ. It consists of two hours taping him each of the last five nights. An attached note informs me that Perez works in a warehouse downtown. He claims that his left leg was severely injured when a load on a forklift tipped over and fell on him. He walks with a severe limp, for which he's collecting workmen's comp. As it happens, a supervisor reported seeing Perez walking in the parking lot without a limp. The warehouse owner hired Total Surveillance to prove that Perez wasn't as badly injured as he claimed.

The clock on the tape shows it's 10:07 on the first night. I press PLAY. The gate of Perez's apartment building opens, and the suspect emerges, walking his German shepherd on a leash. Sure enough, he is hardly limping. He releases the leash, takes a tennis ball out of his pocket, and throws it. The dog chases after it, and Perez breaks into a jog with barely a sign of a limp. I'm annotating the tape to mark the nine-minute segment in which Perez appears when I feel a presence behind me. I pivot my head and see the broad figure of Grant Poole, the CEO of Total Surveillance. Despite the disparity between our positions, Grant and I have always had a strange rapport. I pull off my headphones and swing round to face him.

"We got him," he says.

"It looks that way," I say. "How come you're interested in a small case like this?"

"His boss is a friend of mine. I promised to keep an eye on the case."

"What if the guy argues that he was walking normally on the tape because he took a painkiller?"

Grant laughs. "You're wising up to this business. We'll have to show multiple instances of him walking without a limp to make it stick. Hey, have you ever thought of getting a private investigative license?"

"Um, no offense, but I have no intention of spending half of my nights parked in a car waiting for nothing to happen."

Surprisingly Grant takes no offense at my jab at his profession. "Smart girl. Let me know when you've finished gathering all the evidence on this case, will you?"

"Sure, Grant. Poor guy. He doesn't stand much of a chance when you big boys take an interest."

"I have zero interest in protecting anyone who leeches off my tax dollars. Workers' comp attracts scam artists like pollen does bees." Grant breaks out in a grin. "Keep up the good work."

I spend another hour fast-forwarding through night after night, capturing all the moments in which Perez appears with his dog. Sometimes he shows a pronounced limp; other times he's hardly limping. Who knows if he's scamming his employer?

I spend the next couple of hours on two cases of marital cheating, with no conclusive evidence of sexual contact, just a hand on a waist here or a light kiss on the cheek there.

As I sign out I wonder whether the rest of my evening with Gary will prove any more exciting. I can hear Tricia's voice in my head saying, "Well, now. That's up to you, isn't it?" She's sure got a point, damn her.

*

Surprise! As I let myself into Dave's apartment I find Gary sitting slouched in his friend's armchair, exactly where I always find him. He's wearing torn jeans and an old wrinkled black T-shirt that he probably slept in last night. His ginger hair is done in a ponytail; it looks as if he last shaved a week ago. He is balancing his PlayStation 3 console on his lap, immersed in "Call of Duty 4: Modern Warfare."

"This version is really cool," he greets me. "Instead of taking you back to World War II it takes you into the near future. I'm playing the part of Sgt. Soap McTavish of the SAS, and we are searching for a nuclear device on a cargo ship in the Bering Sea when our ship is fired on by Russian MiGs and begins to sink. I gotta find out how we get out of this one."

Although this greeting is normal, I feel unusually irritated.

I settle down to eat one of two turkey burgers I've brought with me and pass the other to Gary. He accepts it without looking up. I turn on the TV. CSI is on, and it's about a missing person case. I glue my eyes to the screen, hoping for a clue that'll help me find Susan.

When the show ends I turn off the TV. Gary reluctantly puts down his controller and slumps down next to me on the couch that will serve as his bed tonight. He bites into his burger, which must be cold and greasy by now.

"This game's really cool. After we've been hit by Russian MiGs I manage to salvage the cargo manifest of the boat before it sinks. . ."

My mind wanders as he goes on and on. "Now we've found out from his cell phone that he was financed by Zakhaev. So next we're going after him."

"It sounds incredibly Boys' Life to me," I say.

"You chicks just don't get it, do you?"

My irritation flares.

"What don't we chicks get?"

"That this is what men do."

"What? Act like couch potatoes while dreaming that they're Navy SEALs?"

"Forget it!" he snaps. And then, after a brief pause: "Get me a Bud out of the fridge, would you." This doesn't come in the form of a question.

Why don't I tell him to get it himself? Or to go to hell? Instead I get up and bring him a beer. By way of compensation I help myself to one as well. But I still reproach myself for acting like a wimp.

"So," he says. "What you been up to?"

"Susan has disappeared without a trace. Felicia is really worried about her. Today Felicia asked me to find her. She thinks I'm a professional private eye. But I'm not, and I don't know what to do."

Gary thinks for a moment. "Don't you have the Find My Friends app on your phone?"

I nod.

"And do you have her phone number on your app?"

I nod again.

"Well, then," he says disparagingly, "why haven't you given it a try?"

I give it a try. The app says, "NO RESULT FOUND." Susan must have either powered off her cell phone or left it in hidden mode. Too bad.

"You can always try later," Gary says dismissively. He turns to me grinning. "In the meantime we could make out. Take your mind off it."

"You're so romantic," I say sarcastically.

"What's gotten into you today? You're being real bitchy. Don't tell me you've got a headache. Or your period."

"Neither." I can feel myself close to losing my temper.

"Well, then. Here I am. Waiting to be turned on."

Rage seizes me. "Why don't you just rent some porn and make out with yourself?" I snap back angrily.

"How come none of the chicks in my video games are as bitchy as you?" he sneers.

"Because they're created by jerks like you."

"At least they're a turn-on. Unlike you."

Finally I snap. I actually see red. "Then be my guest. Have a party and let *them* turn you on." I jump up, grab my things, and head for the door.

"What the fuck is wrong with you?" Gary shouts at my back.

I turn to face him. "Go back to your zombie half-life. I've had it with you. We're done."

"What do you mean, done?"

"I mean I'm leaving and I'm not ever coming back. Got it now?"

"What have I done to bring this on?"

"Just being yourself. Asshole!"

At the door I take a final look at the shabby apartment with its institutional cream walls, drink-stained sofa, and worn rugs that Gary considers home. Then I storm out of the room, yanking the door shut behind me with a crash.

Standing in the hallway I feel relieved. It's over. Years of being taken for granted by him. Years of pretending he was better than he was. Years of pretending that I was weaker than I am. It's over!

From inside the apartment I hear Gary turning his game back on. I imagine him zapping my avatar on his PS3. Poof! I'm gone in a digital puff of smoke.

*

Driving back to Venice I ask myself, how did he and I ever become an item? We met in my second year at Santa Monica College. In its notorious parking lot where I'd spent an hour that morning cruising, looking for a space until I finally ran out of gas. After pulling over to the side and raising my hood I peered into the engine, fuming. That's when Gary pulled up next to me on his motorbike, told me to hop on the back, and drove me to the nearest gas station, where he filled a gas can he kept stashed in his panier. How unlike him that was. As I later came to discover, life was one long series of unpleasant surprises for him.

But I didn't know that then. So we started dating. Gary was a talented runner, and I traveled with him to lots of races. He always performed well but never won. And no wonder: he often overslept, missed training sessions, and drank too much. How telling. Commitment was not Gary's thing.

Meantime I was studying for an Associate Degree, taking courses in interior design, digital capture, environmental studies, American literature, and Spanish. I took my studies seriously and had a GPA of 3.8. Thanks to Gary, I also had an active social life, partying heavily with the athletic students. Most of the men were jocks and heavy drinkers. Compared to them Gary seemed more my kind of guy—less driven, more casual. Even his drinking seemed restrained compared to theirs. I realize now that this comparison was like measuring the temperature of Venice against the Mojave Desert.

Gary and I started having sex one month after we met. I remember the first time. We were celebrating a win by the track team. A crowd of us ended up plastered in a frat house, when the guys started playing rough, stripping their own clothes, then the women's, until— surprise!—the women found themselves naked while the guys were still wearing their underwear. One couple started having what looked like unprotected sex as the others cheered them on. The remaining guys began to urge the rest of us women to join the action.

I turned to Gary and whispered, "Let's go." Looking at his face, I could see he was turned on. I felt half-repulsed, half turned on myself. Gary had spent the past weeks trying to get me to do more than blow him. It wasn't as if I hadn't lost my virginity in my senior year at high school.

"Can we go all the way?" he asked.

"Yes," I replied, "as long as you've got a rubber."

We jumped on his bike and went to his place. It was all very rushed. We made straight for the bedroom, where I undid his jeans and pulled them to his ankles. Retrospectively I realize this was a mistake, as from then on he expected me to take the initiative every time we had sex.

I also had to undress myself, but I was so over-stimulated by the scene we'd just left that I allowed him to short-circuit the preliminaries. I fitted a condom over his pulsing penis. He immediately thrust it into me and came within a minute.

Disappointing? Maybe. But I was too excited myself to recognize the lack of subtlety until repeated experience made it clear that he was as unpracticed as the other two guys with whom I'd already experienced sex.

I have to admit that for a time Gary's rough, aggressive approach to sex turned me on. It made me feel really wanted, special, desirable. It just shows how deluded you can get when you're needy. I realize now that he would have treated a blow-up doll as well, maybe better, than he treated me.

Why has it taken me so long to wake up to the reality of who Gary is and what our relationship was? Tricia says I lack self-esteem. But then, she goes to workshops and groups like "Building Your Self-Confidence" and "Developing Your Self-Worth" that have basically taught her to put a price tag on her pussy. As Tricia says, "It's your most valuable asset, and it depreciates over time."

For most of the time I really do believe in myself. But when I reflect on how I have related to other people, not just employers but friends and family, I wonder whether I'm not kidding myself. Look at the way I just fetched a beer for Gary instead of telling him to shift his lazy ass and get us both one. I guess I could do with more ego. But Tricia could do with more empathy for other people. Like me, for example.

How much longer am I going to live my life by just getting by? Does it all boil down to money? Is money all that matters? Or that matters most? I refuse to believe that. Sure, it matters. But other things matter as much.

These thoughts are brought to an abrupt halt by arriving home— okay, arriving at Tricia's apartment.

I am greeted by Lulu, who's rubbing herself against my legs, purring loudly. I realize that I'm feeling really down. I raid Tricia's luxurious liquor cabinet and pour myself a generous shot of Herradura Reserva tequila. What will she be doing now? Is she dancing and drinking at a nightclub? Watching her latest date playing blackjack at a casino? Leading him on, then holding out on him?

Wait. What makes me think my life is better than Tricia's? My greatest accomplishment today was finally ending a dead-end relationship with a dead-end dude. I pour a consolation shot into my glass, hoping the tequila will put me to sleep quickly. But not before returning the bottle and washing and putting away the glass.

MIGUEL

Miguel feels even more tired than usual at the end of his shift at Cal Fowl. He takes off his work apron, washes his bloodstained hands and arms, and goes out to collect his bike. He feels lucky—this Friday he has been paid in full for last week's work. Sometimes the pay is late or less than what he is owed. He has a few minutes to spare before biking to Citrus College for his afternoon class in Fundamentals of Automotive Technology.

He refuses to think about his job, but at night his dreams take him back to the processing plant, where he finds himself attaching not chickens but live dogs, cats, birds, even babies to the processing line. The line carries them inexorably down into the vat of electrified water from which they emerge with rigor mortis setting in. To get rid of the dream he will wake himself up and try to conjure up photos of his grandparents' back yard in Oaxaca, where, he's heard, chickens and a rooster spend all day pecking for seeds and insects in the rough grass. But he cannot recall anything of his life back in Oaxaca. All he can remember is what his mother has told him about it. That's because his parents crossed the border when he was an infant. That must be at least twenty-three years ago.

He stops off on the way to the College to grab a pork taco from Taco Nazo, a stand on North Azusa Avenue. Since starting work at Cal Fowl he can't face chicken. He counts out $1.69 in coins and pays the guy. Turning around he bumps into Jesús, a fellow Mexican student from his morning class.

"Hey, hombre, how goes it?" he greets Jesús.

"It's tough, man. You missed the panic here this morning."

"What you talking about?"

"We thought la migra was raiding the stand. RCGT broadcast a warning about two ICE agents seen near the stand. It shut down just as I was about to get my breakfast burrito, and everyone (me included) vanished in seconds."

"Glad you made it out, man."

"It turned out to be a false alarm. Some joker sent out a fake tweet. Followed it up later ranting, 'Kick those wetbacks the fuck out and the fat pigs that gave birth to them.'"

"Bienvenidos a los Estados Unidos de América." They exchange forced grins.

Miguel pays for his taco and soda.

"I'm starving," Jesús exclaims, his mouth stuffed with food.

"That's why you're guzzling two tacos, is it?"

"You try going all day without breakfast."

"What you doing Saturday?" Miguel asks.

"You mean afternoon?"

"Whatever."

"Fishing in the East Fork of the San Gabriel River. And you?"

"A movie."

"With Adela?"

"I'm texting her once I'm done at school."

"She still holding out on you?"

"What can I say? Chicas are all the same."

"No they're not. What's she got that keeps you going back for more?"

"Haven't you noticed? She's got really great breasts." Miguel doesn't think Jesús would appreciate her other non-sexual attractions.

"Keep with it. They all put out in the end."

"You an expert?"

"I just have lower standards."

"Each to his own poison."

"Poison? More like honey."

"Sweet tooth, ha?"

"Best candy I know."

Grinning, Jesús finishes off his second taco and swills it down with a Coke.

Miguel gets back on his bike. "Tonight my mom wants me to join the family after class at Almansor Park."

"El Día de los Muertos?"

"Right. They're making an altar for my aunt. She died in the Sonoran Desert two years ago trying to get back from Oaxaca. Someone slashed the water supply."

"Bad luck." Miguel isn't sure whether Jesús means him or his aunt.

"I miss her."

They both are silent for a moment.

"Got to go to class," Miguel calls back as he cycles off.

"Adiós, amigo."

OCTOBER 30, 2010

I am a small fly caught inside the bedroom ceiling light. I move slowly in starts and stops round the bottom of the translucent glass globe. I am forced to climb over the corpses of other flies that have died in the same fruitless attempt to find a way out. My strength is slowly giving out. Round I go on another futile circuit.

I wake up late. So does Tricia. She's dressed for a workout. Or rather, she's dressed to kill, but at the gym. She's wearing a skintight Spanx black hourglass racerback that hides any trace of cellulite and makes her butt and hips look amazing. The seams make her boobs look bigger and her stomach smaller. Her next-gen Nike high-tech training shoes sync her iPod Nano to her workout app. Of course she has a personal trainer, and of course he electronically tracks her improvements—or the reverse, but these never seem to occur. Oh! She's also wearing her red glitter headband with matching feathers. The total effect has been known to make men at the gym head for the bathroom before their hard-ons show.

She smiles.

Reminds me of a tweet I read recently: "Always smile in the morning; it makes people wonder what you did last night."

"Morning, big sister," I say cheerfully.

"What's so good about it?"

"Actually I didn't say 'good.' For your sake." Here we go.

"So what're you up to today?" she asks, checking out my outfit. For a change I'm smartly dressed in light green cotton skirt, white open-necked blouse, and Mexican espadrilles.

I tell Tricia about Susan's disappearance and my amateur attempts to trace her via my iPhone.

"Have you questioned her landlord yet?" she asks, pouring herself a black coffee.

"Felicia did," I reply sheepishly.

"What kind of a detective accepts hearsay evidence?"

"I guess you're right," I concede. "I'll phone him after I get a coffee."

"Speaking of coffee, I had no trouble making coffee this morning, as the coffee machine was still on the counter from yesterday."

"I'm sorry," I say. Tricia never misses an opportunity to put me down. So, dammit, why do I offer her an avoidable cause?

Lulu rubs up against my legs. Annoyed, Tricia picks her up. Lulu struggles furiously to escape.

"And please don't leave the bag of dirty cat litter outside the door," Tricia adds. "It goes in the trash downstairs, as you know."

"I was late getting to work," I explain lamely. What is the matter with me? I wonder. I just ask for this crap.

"Get up earlier," Tricia says coldly. She sure takes no prisoners.

"Could you ease up on me this morning, please," I say, sensing tears brimming in my eyes. "I'm feeling a bit vulnerable."

"And why is that?" Tricia asks in her idea of a softer tone.

"Because I think I broke up with Gary last night."

"You think?"

"Well, last night I walked out on him. I told him it was finished. My last words were an insult, though whether he understood the sarcasm I'll never know."

"Please don't expect me to commiserate with you," Tricia says coldheartedly. "You should have left that jerk years ago."

Inserting a thin slice of whole wheat bread into the toaster, Tricia adds, "I read a tweet yesterday that could easily have been written by Gary: 'If anyone is near the bathrooms at Muscle Beach can ya toss me a roll under the last stall. Thanks, I'll wait.'"

I can't help laughing. "You could only ever see his faults."

"What else was there to see in that loser?"

"He did have a nice side to him. He was wonderful around animals."

Tricia snorts.

"At any rate—it's over, I think."

"Try to see it positively. Now you're free."

I don't dare admit that I'd rather be captive, though not Gary's.

I really need to lose that wish.

"Don't waste your new freedom getting stuck in another long-term relationship," Tricia adds.

"What do you mean?"

"Haven't you noticed the way men look at you? You've got natural sex appeal. You should make better use of your best assets." She pirouettes to show off her figure.

"And how am I supposed to do that?" I ask skeptically.

"Sex is the one thing all men want. So make them pay top dollar for it. Don't give it away for free. Keep them waiting. Bid up the value of your body." Tricia extracts the slice of toast and smears a smidgen of blueberry jelly on it. "Wait for the really big payoff."

"Payoff?"

"Yes. Gifts. Trips. Meals, of course. Shopping. Jewelry."

"You are unbelievable."

"No, Jenny. I'm a realist. And while I'm offering free advice, remember to always have more than one guy going. It raises your competitive edge. It takes the men you're dating to the next level—from silver to gold." She admires the ring she's wearing today, an opal set in a gold band.

"Do you really think that only men enjoy sex?"

"Of course not. But your own pleasure is a bonus. If you're lucky it comes with the more material returns."

"We never did see life in the same terms," I say. "You make sex sound like a stock purchase. How can I get the best short-term capital return on my body?"

"Now you're starting to get it."

"What happened to affection? Feelings? I won't even bring up love."

"Feelings are dangerous. They prevent you from realizing your full potential—while you still have it."

Tricia glances at the microwave. "Hell. Look at the time. I've got to go."

As she reaches the front door she calls to me over her shoulder, "And don't forget to take the trash downstairs with you." So much for sisterly sympathy.

Tricia exits gracefully, like a student in a ballet class. But then she went to a deportment class. She's also been to a ballet class. She's been to classes in fashion, makeup, social skills, wine appreciation, client relations, investment strategies—to name the ones I remember. And then there was that weekend conference on financial marketing that she made me go to with her. She paid the fees, to be fair. But I had no interest in seminars like "Foreign Exchange Hedging," and "New Cross-Border ACH Formats." It turned out that Tricia wasn't looking for financial know-how. She was looking for a wealthy and reasonably good-looking man in the financial sector to replace the guy she was seeing at the time. Dave was the CEO of a small tech startup business who'd finally offered a big enough bribe to receive the promised reward, which instantly lost half its value. I remember protesting at the end of the weekend about the time wasted being bored out of my mind in order to fish in a pond filled with ugly, well-fed carp. Her only reply: "Better a fat carp than a parasite that lives off of other fish"—meaning Gary. Well, now he's free to fasten onto other fish in the pond.

*

I walk south on Main and turn up Abbot Kinney Boulevard, which has in the past five years turned into LA's trendiest shopping street. Its trajectory is all too familiar. It used to be a derelict strip of rundown beach cottages, artists' studios, and empty brick industrial buildings, unsafe to walk at night. Its few dilapidated stores targeted locals. The yoga studio was plastered with signs promising "NO CHANTING— NO YOGURT—NO SANSKRIT." The shoe repair guy was a Russian émigré, invariably drunk by lunchtime, who returned your shoes looking worse than when you brought them in. Other outlets included a smoke shop with random opening hours, a gay bar, a jazz venue, a newsstand that sold bad coffee on the side, and Surfing Cowboys, the beachwear store.

Today one lone junk clothing store remains, a hand-scrawled notice on its door: "MORE SUNSETS. LESS SELFIES." The tourists love to pose in front of the sign to take—what else?—selfies.

This morning I walk by a Euro-chic eco-friendly organic mattress store, a shoe store advertising "Unique Soles for Unique Souls," an organic brow stylist, whatever that means, a fashionista's window advertising "Design Your Own Custom Clogs," an organic Japanese brown rice sushi bar, and a store offering $100 organic cotton vintage T-shirts "reproduced to the next level." Restaurants offer food that's gluten free and vegan. Bars offer "craft cocktails." Even the real estate office I pass is labeled a "boutique."

I avoid the yuppie techies from Google sipping Americanos at Intelligentsia, where "a barista creates an individualized experience," serving "the most transcendent green beans roasted to perfection." Instead I settle in at Abbot's Habit, a nineteen-year-old coffee shop where the surviving hippies hang out. I order a medium latte for $3.75 and take it to a table where Guy, a musician who works the Boardwalk with his electric guitar, is sitting reading the *LA Times*.

"Hi, Jenny. How's it going?" he asks, looking up from his paper.

I shrug.

"You and me," he says, "we don't count for much these days. What counts is money. Lots of it. I've just been reading about how much Brown and Granger have spent on their campaigns—$188 million up to mid-October. $188 million! I can't even get my head around that sum. And look at this bit of info." Guy points to a heading in the *Times*.

"Between September 1 and October 20 there were 79,000 campaign ads aired just for the governor's race alone," he reads out. "It's disgusting, if you ask me. Not that anyone does. That's because I don't have money. Money matters, I'm telling you."

Of course, he's right.

We continue to chat about the upcoming election while I finish my coffee.

Time to make like a real detective. I say goodbye and walk home.

*

I phone Susan's landlord to make sure he's available, then drive over to meet him. Susan's apartment is the bottom half of a duplex on a quiet Palos Verdes street. The owner lives next door. He turns out to be a fifty-something, overweight, red-faced white guy, wearing a stained white T-shirt emblazoned with the logo NOBAMACARE. He gives off creepy vibes the moment he opens his front door.

"You're Jenny," he greets me with a slight leer.

"Jenny Carter. Pleased to meet you, Mr. Ridley," I say, keeping my distance.

"Call me John. You a friend of Susan's?"

"Actually, I've been hired to investigate her disappearance." I hand him my Total Surveillance business card and take a step back from the sour breath emanating from between his dark yellow teeth.

"Private eyes don't usually come this good looking," he says, ignoring my card, staring at my breasts.

"I'd appreciate you letting me look around her apartment."

"There's nothing to see."

"There's always something to see," I say, sounding like the hardened professional I'm not.

"Follow me, then," Ridley says.

At Susan's front door he unlocks the deadbolt and turns the knob. As it opens, the door sweeps aside the pile of mail on the floor. I pick up the envelopes and rifle through them. Two election mailers, an electricity bill that Ridley reaches out and takes, a solicitation from the Nature Conservancy, and a bunch of junk mail.

"Has the power been cut off yet?" I ask Ridley.

"No. I've been paying for it out of the monthly check."

I look around. Dirty dishes and silverware are piled high in the kitchen sink. An inch of cold coffee sits in the glass pot. The bed is unmade; a red silk nightgown lies on the carpeted floor. The mirrored closet door is open, revealing clothes heaped on the closet floor. No signs of a struggle, apart from a shattered china bowl on the kitchen floor. It looks as if she just left in a hurry and meant to clean things up on her return. As Felicia told me, the plants are dead and withered in their pots.

I go over to the phone machine and press PLAY. A man's voice fills the room.

"Hello, Miss Kirby. My name is Manuel. Mr. Todd Granger asked me to get in touch with you. He gave me something personal to deliver to you. Would you please phone me back to arrange a time when I can drop off the package? My cell phone number is 677-512-3394. Thank you."

I dial the number. It's out of service. Probably a "burner"—a prepaid, disposable cell phone. I make sure the number has registered on my phone, then turn to Ridley, who's watching me from the open doorway.

"Did you see anyone visit her shortly before she disappeared?" I ask.

"I don't spy on my tenants."

"I wasn't suggesting you did."

"She's a looker. She had guys over sometimes." He looks as if he wishes he'd been among them.

"Any visitors in the twenty-four hours before she went missing?"

"I *said*, I don't watch over my tenants' comings and goings."

"Did Susan tell you she was going away?"

"She told me nothing. She kept herself to herself."

I get the impression that he's mad at her for some reason.

"Did you ever ask her out?" I ask.

"Not my type," he answers.

"You called her a looker."

"She always gave me the cold shoulder."

"She could be distant," I say, hoping to bolster his ego.

"She didn't have your figure," he responds, once more fixated on my breasts. He pulls out a wrinkled used tissue, vigorously twists it around in his nostrils, and inspects the results intently.

"So you're still getting her monthly rent checks?"

"Yeah. Twenty-fifth of the month. Transferred into my account, regular as clockwork."

"You bank online?"

"Yeah."

"I'd like to see your bank statements, please."

"That would depend," he says, leering at me.

"On what?" I ask unsuspectingly.

"On what you would be willing to give in return." He appears to be fixated on my cleavage.

Oh god! I should have known this guy was twisted.

"Can't we keep this simple?" I ask without much hope of a positive response.

"Look, lady. I'm not asking much. Just a look and a memento."

"What exactly are you suggesting?" I say guardedly. I'm only prepared to do so much for the info.

"All I want is to take a photo of you. I'm a sucker for good lookers. I've got a whole collection of lookers like you."

There is a long pause. "Alright. I'll do it after we've looked at those checks. But nothing else. No touching. We understand each other?"

This can't be what Tricia had in mind when she advised me to use my assets.

"Whatever you say," he replies grinning.

We go back to his cream-colored living room. He sits down at his laptop and brings up his Bank of America account.

"There's the latest check deposit." He passes me his laptop.

I click on "View Images." The check, dated October 25, was written for $2,200 on the account of SUSAN KIRBY. 1522 BROOKS AVENUE, VENICE, CA 90291. The signature is illegible. I know that Brooks Avenue doesn't extend east of Lincoln, so I also know the address is a fake. This is a dead end. Now I have to pay my part of the bargain.

"Thanks for showing me this. So where do you want me to pose for you?"

"How about lying down on the couch?" he asks as he eagerly grabs his Nikon.

"I don't think so," I respond, thinking of how vulnerable that position would make me. "How about here by the computer?"

"I guess that'll do," he says grudgingly. I lean back in the chair.

"Half turn round so that the sunlight coming through the window slats falls on your front," he instructs me, becoming more his true self.

I do as he asks.

"Great! Now hold it," he says with a croak in his voice. He snaps one take after another. In the corner of my eye I become aware of a swelling in his pants. I jump up and grab my clothes.

"Hang on," he says. "I'm not yet done."

"You're done," I say. "And I'm done too," I add as I make quickly for the door. Happily, there's no one to witness my flight.

I drive off feeling smirched and ashamed of myself. Surely a good private eye would have managed to extract such simple information without offering favors in return. I can't blame it on my gender. Tricia would never have made such a deal. Does this mean that I'm lacking self-esteem? Should I be taking some of those courses Tricia is addicted to that I have been so scathing about? Now I'm being ridiculous. There has to be another way of interacting with my world that is not just an acquired technique. Somehow I need to insert myself and my needs into situations like this one. But how?

*

I am sitting in my old Corolla a few blocks away from Mr. Creepy filled with confusion and anger—more at myself than at the jerk I've just left. How could I have put myself into such a potentially risky position? For all I know he could be listed online as a convicted sex offender.

To distract myself I start fiddling with my iPhone. I look at my Facebook page and see a notification number that of course draws me in to the spell of the app. It's Amy inviting her "friends" to join her at the farmer's market in Santa Monica. I know she's not going there to buy anything as real as fruit or vegetables. She updates her status all the time because no one otherwise is going to ask her what she's doing. All she gets in response are pokes.

Now I'm sounding as if I belonged to my parents' generation. I really enjoy Facebook. And YouTube. Yet I resent the pressure to compete in this popularity contest—one more way of living out your life as if you were a character acting a part onstage. What I object to is the lack of authenticity. I want to be myself, whatever that is, not some staged persona.

Wow! Here's Gary: "Hey everyone. I've changed my status. I'm SINGLE again. I took the L from LOVER. I'm hot. Get ready for HOOKUP." I have to admit I feel a pang of jealousy at the thought of another woman making out with him. What a fool I am. Be thankful, I tell myself, to have your life back. Now do something with it. That doesn't mean look for meaning in another relationship. I want my own life. I want to feel fully committed to what I am and do. I want to be involved with others, but not dependent on them for validation, like Amy.

I decide to unfollow and unfriend Gary. At least that is doing something for myself.

Two years ago Gary and I agreed to try a trial separation—not that we ever lived together. It was Gary who'd suggested the time apart. Of course it was. It turned out his motivation was the teenage sister of a friend of his, whose house was his latest crash pad. He had just enough morality to stop cheating outright on me, but he'd already done everything short of fucking her before suggesting the convenient time apart.

At the time, I decided to take the opportunity to try dating someone who was actually successful. So I signed on to Match.com. The hilarious screen names guys used—1Up; Apathesis (Gary should have used that one); Pessifist; Bad Glands; Sindromo; King Pong; Low Bald; Str8up; and—most off-putting of all—Xcreta!

As for the photos, I quickly lost count of the number of men holding a beer bottle in one hand and a gun in the other—or a sword, or the handlebars of a Harley-Davidson. Then there were the bare-from-the-waist, muscle-flexing types, clearly already having passionate love affairs with themselves. A few were obviously cropped couple photos with the guy's arm going off frame—big turnoff.

The profiles offered the best clues to whom or what I was dealing with. The clichés—loves sharing; affectionate and considerate; warm heart; has a passion for barbecuing; loves hiking/baseball/drinking. The spelling and grammar—your welcome; its four you; there going to love you. The abbreviations—dont msg me if u luv urself; LOL; SO; OMG. The autocorrects: How about a playmate (playdate)? Czech this image. It's all the fault of autoerect.

Eventually I got into a text exchange with a guy named Eric who seemed reasonably attractive and demonstrated enough humor to make me want to learn more. Our match was around 90 percent. He wrote that he liked to hike in the Santa Monica Mountains and read his favorite author—Philip Roth. That sounded promising. But how could I get him to suggest a date without seeming pushy? After confessing that I was no hiker, I mentioned that on Fridays I often stopped in at Chez Jay's for a margarita. He promptly texted, "Let's meet there this Friday. Will 5 work for you?"

He arrived half an hour late, looking nothing like his photo. He must have been at least in his mid-forties. His hair was thinning, and he needed glasses to read the menu. If he'd been hiking it must have been after dark; his pale skin showed no sign of having encountered the sun. He also had a facial twitch that soon got on my nerves. Unfair, I know. But I couldn't help it.

He chose a table that gave him a clear line of sight to the TV that was tuned to a football game with USC playing some team from Oregon. He spent more time watching the screen than looking at me. Eric ordered filet mignon and lobster tail for himself and, before I could open my mouth, he ordered Caesar salad with shrimp for me. When I shot him an incredulous look, he explained, "My mother always orders that. She swears by it."

It went downhill from there. Next his cell phone rang and he took time out to talk to his mother: "Can we talk about this later? You don't know her . . . of course I will." Subsequently, as the waiter stopped by to ask us what drink we would like next, I was saying how much I liked *Zuckerman Bound*. "I'll have one of those," he told the waiter. He couldn't have got very far reading Roth. No sooner had we extricated ourselves from that fracas than his mother was on the phone again: "I told you, I'm having a meal . . . What's not good enough for you? I'll be home by 8:30 at the latest." A minute later his face lit up as USC scored a touchdown. He showed more animation watching the game than at anything I could say or do.

When his cell phone rang a third time I didn't wait for him to answer. "Maybe you should have dinner with your mother instead," I said. Throwing a twenty onto the table, I stormed out of the place.

When I got home Tricia said, "You should have asked to change places with him to cut him off from the TV, and after the first phone call suggested a moratorium on calls. Still, he clearly wasn't worth that much effort. I'd have downed my margarita and told him he was a jerk as I left. And never pay for the first meal unless you really like the guy." On the ball, as always—and ruthless, of course.

Two weeks later Gary was back. I was happy to settle for the devil I knew. Bad choice, it turns out.

*

My phone rings as I am staring at it, trying to figure out how to tell Felicia what I'd found at Susan's apartment, and my conclusion that something is terribly wrong.

There's a coincidence. It's Felicia.

"Jenny? That you?"

"Hi, Felicia. What's up?"

"You have time to drop by the house?" She sounds strained. "Is urgente."

"I guess I could if it's really urgent. I'm in Palos Verdes. Why?"

"I can't say you on the phone. It's personal. Please. Ven!"

"Okay. I'm on my way."

"Muchas gracias, amiga. I'll have a salad ready. Hasta pronto."

*

Felicia greets me at Todd's back door, dishcloth in hand. She is flustered. We hug. I feel enveloped by her warmth and love.

"You looking smart," she says looking me up and down.

"I just went to Susan's apartment."

"What you find?"

"I'm sorry to disappoint you, but nothing good."

"What you mean?" Felicia asks fearfully.

"The owner showed me images of the last rent check he'd received, supposedly from her."

"Supposedly? Why you say that?"

"Because it came from a phony address."

"What has happened to her?" Felicia demands. "I miss her so much." Tears fill her eyes.

"I don't know. Something weird is going on, for sure." I realize I am deeply troubled by the false address on the check.

"I know it was no right." Felicia thumps the kitchen counter with exasperation.

Despite feeling shaken myself, I try to calm her down. "It certainly is suspicious, but there is no evidence so far that Susan has come to any harm."

"Harm," Felicia almost shouts. "Why does a person want to hurt her?"

"They wouldn't. There is probably a perfectly ordinary explanation for her disappearance. Like she was so hurt by the breakup that she went overseas somewhere."

"I hope you right," Felicia says, grasping at this straw I offer her. "I know you find her soon," she says, reassuring herself.

She means it. It's my problem now.

After a long pause she says, "Come and have some lunch."

Felicia and I sit down on stools at the wooden kitchen counter where she has put out a bowl of mixed salad, sliced green chorizo from Toluca, and a small bowl of chipotle chilies in adobo sauce. She takes a basket of warmed-up tortillas from the oven and pours a cold lemon drink from a glass jug into two green recycled glass tumblers.

"Que aproveche!" Felicia appears to have regained her equilibrium.

"So what's so secret you can't tell me on the phone?" I ask.

"Eat some chiles. They're specialty." Now she's teasing me by delaying her story.

"Todd's not home?"

"No. Señor Granger is with that antipático brother of his at an election meeting in Irvine."

"The anti-immigration rally?"

Felicia nods. "They say blood stronger than water."

"Thicker."

"What?"

"The saying is, 'Blood is thicker than water.'"

"Why do Señor Granger appear with people who hate immigrants?"

"I have no idea." Like Felicia, I cannot connect the Todd who supports Felicia with the guy who's bankrolling Dan's hate campaign. It just doesn't add up. Todd seems to have a heart of gold. And yet he allies himself with a party that wants to punish unions, get rid of public services for the poor, and deport undocumented immigrants.

"What was it you wanted to tell me?" I ask.

"I was cleaning the kitchen this morning," she answers. "I picked up the picture of Mr. Todd with Susan in Fiji, with the buttons on it—"

She looks at me questioningly. "The digital picture frame?" I say.

She nods. "By mistake I push one button and it make a noise. I pressed another button to try to stop it and you know what?"

"What?"

"It was a movie of me talking yesterday to Quan, the pool maintenance jornalero, here in the kitchen. But it wasn't a movie. It was the real conversation."

I give this a moment's thought. "I find it hard to believe that Todd would use a nanny cam on you" I say. "He trusts you completely."

"Watch it." Felicia gets up and fetches the framed photo.

I press the PLAY button and see Felicia pouring a glass of water for Quan. She says, "I know you don't drink so clean." She means non-alcoholic. She's flirting with him.

Quan replies in a similar tone: "Why would I need anything stronger, when I have you for company?"

Felicia laughs.

"Thank you for the water," Quan says and leaves the kitchen.

"It's a motion-detector video camera," I say. "This is something I know about. It must have an SD card inside." I turn it round, open the back, and take out the secure digital memory card. These cards that are barely an inch long are portable and can carry an awful lot of data. "On my other job I spend my evenings fast forwarding through these things."

"Why Señor Granger do this to me?" Felicia wails.

"I don't know."

"I trust him. He trust me."

"I know. It makes no sense."

I turn the SD card over. I recognize the label on the back. It's one of Total Surveillance's. I take out my iPhone and copy the serial number.

"This belongs to the company I work for," I tell Felicia. "I'm going there this evening. I'll check it out."

Felicia looks bewildered.

"Maybe I can find who commissioned this in the company records," I say reassuringly.

"Espero que sí."

"I hope so, too."

I replace the card, rewind it to where it last stopped playing, and press ERASE to eliminate the record of my visit and my conversation with Felicia about the device.

*

I need a break. I park on Larkspur and scramble down the slope to Corona del Mar State Beach. On this beautiful Saturday, the beach is crowded with families enjoying this stretch of sand and sea. At the same time it has a secluded, private feel to it, being walled in on one side by the cliffs and on the other by the rock pier that forms the east entrance to Newport Harbor. Every firepit is occupied, some by families, others by groups of what look like UC Irvine students.

I walk south to the rocky, less crowded section of the beach. The tide is coming in. I linger over the tide pools, crystal clear and alive with small anemones, crabs, snails, and monster-size starfish. I wonder what it must feel like spending your life clamped to a rock, exposed to the sun and stars. The repetition of the waves must be so reassuring. My own existence doesn't seem to amount to anything more. Am I better or worse off being able to think about it? Why do we assume there has to be some purpose to our life? Or if, like Tricia, you think it has no purpose, how do you find the motivation to go on with it all? What's the point of it?

I'm cursed with my parents' outlook, which insists on examining all sides of any issue. All that does is leave me ambivalent.

Well, not always. What is worse than ambivalence is the alternative: close-mindedness and prejudice. Dan's extreme stand on immigration, for example. You can only adopt that stance if you have no empathy for others. I prefer ambivalence to that any day.

Still, too much sympathy can leave my wants and needs out altogether. Look at Mom. She has spent her life sacrificing herself to Dad, Tricia, and me, and all those social causes that Dad has chosen for both of them. This has turned her into a product of endless repressions with no core sense of herself. No wonder she seems lost much of the time.

*

Why would Todd want to secretly spy on Felicia (or maybe all of us), I wonder some time later, as I drive back to Tricia's apartment once more. Is he more paranoid than he gives out? Has another employee accused Felicia of stealing? He couldn't possibly believe that. Or did he set up surveillance in the kitchen because he suspects someone else? He is after all a CEO. It's true that CEOs are some of the most ruthless assholes in America. Yet Todd doesn't come across as one. I'm baffled.

The NPR news on the car radio interrupts my thoughts:

"Republican gubernatorial nominee Dan Granger admitted today that he had employed Alfonso Gomez, a worker without documentation, to help in the construction of an apartment above the garage of his house. 'I only discovered his status after he fell off a scaffold and injured his back in late September,' State Senator Granger declared. 'I reported him to the U.S. Immigration authorities, and he was deported shortly after.'"

"Contacted in Guadalajara, Mexico, Gomez claimed that the senator knew he was illegal five months ago after he received a letter from the Social Security Administration advising him that Gomez's social security number didn't match. Asked what help Gomez had received following the injury, Gomez told our reporter that the senator had paid his cab fare to the emergency room. After that, the senator refused to have any further contact, refusing to pay the earnings he owed Gomez. 'Senator Granger treated me like a piece of garbage,' Gomez said. 'I was thrown away once I was no more use to him.'"

"In his debate with the Democratic gubernatorial nominee yesterday, Senator Granger said that employers should be held accountable for hiring undocumented workers."

So he's not just a slime ball, but a hypocrite as well. Not to mention heartless. How could that creep be the brother of Todd? I suppose the same question could be asked about Tricia and me. As different as night and day.

*

When I get back to Venice in the early afternoon I decide to indulge myself. It's Saturday, after all. I head for my favorite gallery, LA Louver, which has a new mixed show of figurative painting by well-known sixties artists like Hockney, Diebenkorn, and Kossoff. I circle round the stark main gallery with its white walls and polished concrete floors, lingering in front of the paintings that capture my eye. I realize that almost every painted female figure appears to be either isolated from her surroundings, or distrustful of what she is looking at. Charles Garabedian shows a nude Jean Harlow in an unrecognizable landscape pointing her index finger at some unattainable object just beyond the frame of the canvas. Leon Kossoff's *Nude on a Red Bed* depicts her huddled on a flat red platform of a bed with a yellow splash for a pillow and a fawn-colored backdrop. There are no consoling objects, no lamps or chairs draped with discarded clothes. Just a cowering naked woman robbed of any sense of self. Even Rebecca Campbell's painting of a mother lying on a bed holding a baby and grasping a young boy by the hand shows her gazing into space, not at them, with apprehension.

Have we women always felt ultimately alone in the universe? Vulnerable, fearful, perpetually in danger? Why do I feel so alienated from my friends and family? I cannot identify either with my parents' continual self-sacrifices, or with Tricia's obsessive pursuit of money as the only route to happiness, and to hell with the rest of us. Now that I think about it, I felt lost and lonely throughout my childhood. My friends all seemed to find some security in their families. But I could never share my feelings of vulnerability with either of my parents. They were too wrapped up in one another's life. And Tricia had already embarked on a lifetime battle with the world—including me.

I remember one occasion when my history teacher in high school accused me of plagiarism. She told me that an essay I had turned in on

Abraham Lincoln was too sophisticated for someone my age. She gave me twenty-four hours to come up with an explanation of where I had obtained the material. When I told my parents what she had said, my mother wouldn't take the charge seriously and just laughed. My father actually sided with the teacher, asking what sources I'd used. As for Tricia, she advised me to tell the teacher to get lost. Eventually I solved my problem by myself. I entered my essay in an online plagiarism checker, and it came up blank. When I showed this to the teacher, she just said, "It seems I underestimated your abilities." No apology. My point is that any of my friends would have had an irate parent in the principal's office demanding that the teacher apologize and be disciplined.

So I grew up feeling I was on my own. And yet I was convinced that this was not natural. We all need some support from those close to us. This sense of isolation only made me try harder to embrace others, to offer them what I was missing. That in turn has led me to constantly put myself last. No one is going to give me a prize for that. Yet working for a cause has always fulfilled me more than working just for the sake of the money. I believe that it is possible to please yourself while working for the well-being of others.

I think of David Hockney's painting of Mike Izzo in the exhibition. Behind the seated young man is the reflection of him from the rear and behind him the reflection of Hockney seated at his easel painting him. That's what the other painters omitted—their own relation to the sitters. Relationships matter to me. I won't live my life as Tricia does—

one woman battling the rest of the world. The portrayal of women as isolated and at war is itself a half-truth, a perspective created by men.

Baffled by these thoughts, I let myself into the apartment—I notice I cannot get myself to say "my" or even "our," even though I pay Tricia rent—and raid the fridge for a cookie and lemonade.

*

It's almost 6 pm as I drive into the Total Surveillance underground parking lot. I swore I'd stop comparing myself to Tricia, but I can't help juxtaposing the evening each of us is about to experience. Ralph, an ex-client to whom Tricia sold a three-million-dollar house on the Venice canals, netting her more money than I earn in three years, is taking her to Leap of Faith, a musical starring Raúl Esparza and Brooke Shields. Before the show, they're having dinner at Kagaya, an expensive shabu-shabu restaurant in Little Tokyo. Not that Tricia will be *eating* the shabu-shabu beef (she counts each day's calorie intake). She told me she'll stick to tofu soup, steamed fish and green tea mousse. Washed down with lots of top-quality chilled sake, of course. After the show they'll go back to his place on Linnie Canal for a nightcap and "the payoff" as she calls it.

I, on the other hand, will spend the evening fast-forwarding through hours of surveillance tapes, trying to identify sordid moments of criminal or immoral conduct. Wouldn't I rather be doing what Tricia's doing tonight? Well, no. But I *would* rather be going to the Halloween party I had to turn down at my friend Alice's, which my work is preventing me from attending. Alice is incredibly social. She seems to know everyone in Venice. She's divorced and appears to be happily self-sufficient and self-confident. Unlike me, she says what she thinks and still remains friends with those she speaks the truth to. She's my role model, but I have no idea how to transform myself to be more like her.

As I park my car in a space reserved for Total Surveillance, I notice that Grant's gleaming black BMW 531i is still there. I guess a CEO has to work overtime occasionally to earn his annual salary of over a million dollars plus bonuses and stock options. Grant seems to be a nice guy, but he must have a ruthless side to be where he is.

I have given myself enough time before my shift to first stop by the registry. The registry is a soulless, windowless room filled with metal filing cabinets that should have been replaced by digital storage years ago. I ask the duty clerk, looking bored behind a desk littered with papers, to get me the records, which are ordered numerically. So it's easy to find the card I copied in Todd's kitchen: #4357: 399 BAY ISLAND—KITCHEN.

To my surprise there's more. Another ten devices are listed at the same address, in the living room, den, dining room, office, three bedrooms, and three bathrooms. The entire house has been bugged.

What the hell is Todd doing? Is he paranoid? Why would he want to tape the everyday comings and goings of his family, friends, and staff?

Could it have something to do with Susan's disappearance?

All the cards were activated a day after Susan left Todd. Does he suspect that someone in the household has something to do with

Susan's disappearance? Alternatively, could he be responsible himself for her disappearance? I'm baffled. A private eye who lacks eyesight.

I leave the records department and lock myself in my viewing booth, where at least I know what I'm looking for.

On my worktable lies the card for RAUL PEREZ. There's a Post-it stuck to it that says, "Please deal with this one first. Grant." I insert the card into the digital player, slip on my headphones, and turn my iPod to *The Fame Monster*. Lady Gaga opens with "Oh, caught in a bad romance." Some bloggers say that Gaga's bad romance is with fame. I relate it to my experience with Gary.

I become aware of Grant hovering behind me, watching the tape on fast-forward over my shoulder.

I press STOP and remove my earphones.

"Evening, Grant," I greet him. "Isn't it kind of late for you to be here?"

"I just wanted to check whether Perez was caught on video running with the dog again last night. I promised my friend who employs him that I'd phone him tomorrow morning with news of how much evidence he has to use against him."

"I was just getting to the time he takes the dog out on the tape when I stopped it."

"Let's have a look at it now, so I can go home."

I press FAST FORWARD. As soon as Perez appears on the monitor at his front gate with the dog, I press PLAY. He's limping badly. When he throws the ball for his dog he stays where he is until the dog returns the ball to his feet, when he stiffly reaches down to pick it up.

"This time he appears much more impeded than the previous day. Why is nothing ever black or white in this business?" Grant says. "I'll have to advise the client to select which tape segments to use, and then the outcome will depend on whether Perez is given a lawyer smart enough to demand all the segments."

"The difference in his mobility might just be because he took a painkiller in the earlier segment, and not in this one."

"He's just a lazy jerk in my book."

Another conservative CEO who thinks every poor American on public assistance is robbing them. I change the subject.

"You're a friend of Todd Granger's, aren't you?" I ask.

"We meet for lunch from time to time."

"You know I take care of his plants?"

"No. You never told me. You're a girl of many talents."

"Yesterday when I was talking to Todd's housekeeper she asked me why he was taping her in the kitchen. I took a look at the SD card hidden in a digital picture frame. It was one of ours. What puzzles me is why Todd would want to bug his own house."

"He wouldn't," Grant says.

"Then who would?" I ask.

Grant instantly recovers his professional persona. "I have no idea. And if I did, I'd be breaking client privilege to talk about it with you." He clearly regrets his momentary slip.

I feign nonchalance. "Not important. Just wondering."

"I've got to get going. I'm due at a charity dinner at the Standard in ten minutes."

"I hope the food's good," I say.

"Goodnight," he calls as he leaves.

"Bye," I call back.

How, I ask myself, can I find out who paid Total Surveillance to bug Todd's house? And whether the bugging has anything to do with Susan's disappearance . . . I know.

I take the elevator to the third floor and let myself into Grant's empty outer office, where he keeps all the client files. The cabinets are organized alphabetically by location—Newbury Park; Newhall; Newport Beach. I pull open the drawer. The files are sequenced by streets—Balboa Blvd; Bay Ave; Bay Island. I pull out the bulky pocket file for 399 Bay Island and extract the contract:

"This agreement is made on this August 3, 2010, between Jorge Valdez of 2410 Imperial Avenue, San Diego, CA 92102, hereinafter Debtor, and Total Surveillance Inc. of 10252 Santa Monica Boulevard, Los Angeles, CA 90067, hereinafter Secured Party . . ." I am entering the name and address of the client in my iPhone when Alexandro Perez, the security officer, bursts through the door.

"Oh! It's you, Jenny."

"Hi, Alexandro," I greet him with a smile. "What's up?"

"You set off the alarm when you opened the filing cabinet."

"I'm sorry. I must have entered the wrong code." In fact, I'd forgotten I needed to deactivate the alarm before opening the drawer.

"That's okay. Beats sitting staring at those security screens all night."

"I should be done here in an hour or so."

"Bueno. Drop by on your way out."

"Will do."

He leaves, and I use my iPhone to take a copy of the contract, then turn to the trove of SD cards in the file. I separate those labeled kitchen, living room, dining room, office, and den, and make copies of all of them. I return the file to its drawer and go back to my booth on the first floor, where half a dozen more cards from other cases wait to be played and annotated.

As I'm leaving the office later, I phone Alice.

"Hi, sweetheart, "she says. "I knew it was you."

"I've just left work."

"At 10 pm?"

"I know," I sigh. "Is your party still going?"

"Everyone except Bruno left at least an hour ago."

"And who's Bruno?" I ask teasingly.

"He's an immigrant from Brazil. Overstayed his tourist visa. Now he's in hiding."

"And you're no doubt helping keep him hidden?"

"You could say that."

"I sense an ulterior motive. Handsome?"

"Gorgeous. I'm looking at him as I say this."

"In that case I'll let you go. Have a great evening—or should I say night?"

I end the call, feeling sorrier for myself than ever.

MIGUEL

Miguel wakes up, rolls over, and glances at the clock radio on the nightstand next to him. He is stunned to realize he'd slept till 12:23 pm. It's worth it, he decides. For the first time in a week he feels well rested. The floor of his tiny bright-yellow bedroom is littered with the clothes he threw off last night, two empty beer cans, some textbooks, a file of loose papers, a Lakers pennant, and a dented black toolbox.

"Mamá! What's for breakfast?" he calls out through the door.

"Get your lazy butt in here and you'll see," she calls back.

After a quick shower, Miguel stands staring at his closet. What figure does he want to present to the world this Saturday? He selects dark gray clinging chinos and a light gray zip-up vest with a crest logo. Yes, he decides, nothing but shades of white, black, and gray. So he pulls out of his drawer a black long-sleeved T-shirt and chooses white sneakers to complete the effect.

"Off to see El Presidente?" his mother teases him as he enters the kitchen.

"How did you know? The limousine will be here at 1." He pours himself a cup of coffee and watches his mom cook his favorite breakfast dish—sausage-and-egg tacos. Having browned and crumbled the sausage she pours beaten egg into the skillet and stirs the mixture till it's done. After taking out two heated tortillas from the microwave she fills them with some of the mixture, sprinkles on grated cheese and cilantro, and rolls them up. Miguel adds salsa and sour cream and bites into the first one.

"Great, Mamá."

"You're so appreciative this morning," his mother says. "You must want something."

"How about no more deportations?"

"We should be so lucky."

"Where's everyone?" Miguel asks.

"Unlike you, they got up this morning. Your sister is helping Aunt Teresa clean the Enderbys' house. Dad took the car to the shop."

"You mean Dad's being ripped off by those two crooks at Silva Auto Repairs again?"

"You need to go easy on your papa. You know he's not well. All that dust from the weed whacker and leaf blower brings on his asthma."

"How can I not know? He tells us at least once a day."

"Don't be like that. He has such a tough time with his breathing."

"Then why doesn't he do something about it?"

"Like what?"

"Like go to the ER?"

"You're crazy. They'd ask for his ID."

"Anyone knows they don't do that. Anyway, that wasn't what I was talking about. I just don't understand why he lets those dudes at the shop rip him off all the time."

"We can't do without a working car, mijo. Finish your tacos before they get cold." She slides two more freshly made tacos onto his plate. "Where are you off to?"

"I'm taking Adela to the movies."

"You're treating her?"

"Of course."

"Why can't she pay for herself?"

"Oh, Mamá! If I like her, why can't you at least like her for my sake?"

"I just don't trust her. She uses you," she responds.

"You say that about every girl I've ever dated." Looking at his watch, Miguel says "Gotta go," grabs his bike lock and quickly leaves the house.

*

Emerging from the Regency Foothill Cinema in Azusa where they'd seen *The Girl Who Kicked the Hornets' Nest*, Miguel and Adela stand blinking in the blinding afternoon sun.

"I don't think it was as good as the last one," says Miguel.

"I liked it better," Adela says. "Less blood."

Adela looks up at him with her large beautiful eyes. Miguel loses interest in their budding argument.

"Can we get a frozen yogurt at Pinkberry?" she suggests. "It's right here, and I love their pomegranate mango swirl—"

"And I love the swirl you put me in," Miguel says flirtatiously.

"Oh, come on with you," she says, blushing.

They drift into Pinkberry's clean, bright space with its soothing air-conditioning and join the line.

Suddenly three men with handguns drawn burst into the store. They're wearing T-shirts with ICE emblazoned across the front. One of the agents roughly pushes Miguel and Adela aside and jumps the counter.

"Everyone stay where you are and don't move," he yells. "Don't move!"

He turns to the two young women behind the counter: "Give me your papers. Now!"

One of the women reaches for her purse. The other freezes in place, visibly shaking. Then she makes a dash for the rear exit. The ICE agent easily grabs her from behind and throws her face down on the floor. Then he forces his knee into her back and puts his full weight on it. She screams.

"Stop it!" Miguel shouts. "She's not resisting you."

The agent forces the woman's arms together behind her back. The other agent thrusts his face into Miguel's. "Who do you think you are? The Dark Knight? Show me your papers. NOW!"

"As soon as you stop brutalizing that woman," Miguel says.

"Your papers!" the agent demands. "Quick!"

Miguel reaches into his back pocket for his papers.

"Slowly does it," says the agent, obviously fearing a weapon.

"I thought you just said 'Quick!'" Miguel says as he hands the agent his papers.

"Don't get clever with me," the agent says. "Hands behind your back."

Miguel complies. The agent grabs his hands and cuffs him.

"What are you doing?" Miguel sputters. "You asked me for my papers. I gave them to you."

"You'll have to come with us while we check out this social security number," the agent announces. He appears to enjoy throwing his weight around.

"Where are you taking him?" Adela asks. Miguel glances at her and sees tears streaming down her face.

"Downtown."

"Where downtown?" she demands.

"Please step away from the officer," the third agent tells Adela. The one who handcuffed Miguel shoves him out the front door and into a dark SUV marked ICE that's idling at the curb. The first agent manhandles the young woman who tried to run into the back next to Miguel. She and Miguel are seated with one agent between them. The other two agents get in the front seats, and the driver takes off with a screech of tires.

SUNDAY,
OCTOBER 31, 2010

I start my Sunday, orange juice in hand, with my weekly call to Mom.

"Hello, sweetheart. How are you?" she asks, as she does every Sunday.

"Oh, okay. Well actually I'm feeling a little fragile today."

"And why is that?" Mom immediately suspects the worst.

"I broke up with Gary," I blurt.

After a pause, Mom says, "I'm sorry to hear that."

"No, you're not. You never really liked him."

"I did think he should have offered to marry you before now."

"You do know that more Americans are unmarried than married?"

"That doesn't make them any happier, does it?" Touché.

"Tricia thinks it's the best thing I've done in a long time."

"Your sister never did see things the way you do."

"You can say that again."

"She's well?"

Tricia rarely calls home.

"She's doing great. The housing market is picking up. Last week she closed a deal for a million-five."

"My goodness! And you, dear?"

"I still have my two part-time jobs."

"That's something these days. And how's Gary?"

"Mom! I just told you, we broke up."

"I'm sorry to hear that," she says, unaware of repeating herself. "I told you that Dad had his overtime cut off completely last month, didn't I?"

"Yes, Mom." What the hell?

After a pause, Mom says, "I saw Dr. Snow last week. Or was it yesterday?"

Uh-oh.

"And . . .?"

"He said I'm suffering from depression."

"That doesn't sound like you."

"I've been trying to keep my thoughts to myself. Your father's got enough worries as it is."

"What worries?" I ask.

"He's worried that he may be let go." Even my mother is using one of corporate America's more absurd euphemisms. As if employees have been dying to be released and a corporation has reluctantly agreed to their wishes.

Mom continues, "He's been talking about moving to Oakland."

"Oakland?"

"I mean Oklahoma."

"Oklahoma! Why Oklahoma of all places?"

"An old college buddy of his now works at this nonprofit in Oklahoma City—"

"What nonprofit?"

"It's called the African American Health Board something or other. His friend says they are looking for—what was it?—an advocate in social action."

"How's the pay?"

"About the same as what he's getting now. But they have no restrictions on overtime."

"And do you want to move to Oklahoma?"

Mom starts crying. "All my friends live here," she says between sobs.

"Have you told Dad how you feel?"

"I tried. But he's so excited about starting a new mission in Oakland."

"Oklahoma." I correct her a little unkindly. Is Mom going senile? "It's not a mission. It's just another job, Mom."

"He sees it differently. It's about improving the lives and health of the poor. I feel selfish putting my friends before his career."

"What about *your* life?"

"You don't understand, Jenny. It's complicated."

"Yes, it's complicated because it involves you as well, not just Dad."

"Oh dear, I'm going to have to hang up. Your father just got home from walking the dog."

"We'll talk about this again, Mom."

"We'll see, dear. Goodbye for now."

"Bye, Mom."

What a mess. Is Dad going through a late midlife crisis? He's normally so evenhanded. Family! Hell for children, as Strindberg said.

*

After I've had breakfast on my own at home, I shut myself in my bedroom to go through the SD cards I copied. I had planned to spend the morning at the Santa Monica farmers market on Main Street. It's a cool place, combining fresh produce—organic, of course, as it's Santa Monica—with stalls selling cooked artisan foods, and a mix of local retail outlets and artist vendors. Families watch their kids having their faces painted, or taking pony rides, or petting farm animals. But this Sunday I am forced to give all that a miss.

The fifth card is a recording of Todd's living room. And here's Todd talking to a Mexican-looking guy. I switch to PLAY mode:

". . . the question is, Jorge," Todd says as he pours out a whiskey and hands it to him, "how clean are the sources of the money you're investing in my company?"

Jorge, I recall, is the name on the surveillance contract. Jorge is Spanish for George, so the name is common as mud. How likely is it that he is the same Jorge who signed the contract?

This Jorge looks like he's in his early fifties, with pale skin, black hair, piercing eyes, and a black Pancho Villa moustache. He's wearing a smart white shirt with a plain dark-blue tie over loose black linen pants, and a huge silver signet ring on his right middle finger. He speaks impeccable English.

"No problem. The money is legit. It comes from our racing stable in Galveston."

"A billion dollars? Legit?" Todd asks skeptically.

"You don't know the racing game well, I take it?"

"No. I only gamble on the stock market," Todd laughs.

"Champion horses sell for millions of dollars. As for betting, more than a hundred million dollars is bet on the Kentucky Derby alone. It doesn't take much to reach a billion in the racing business."

"By fixing races? Doping horses?"

"We don't need to resort to tactics like that to make our money."

"Which doesn't mean that you don't do so."

"Even if we did, you wouldn't want to know that."

"Okay. Okay. Make the electronic transfer first thing in the morning. And don't forget the $100,000."

What's he talking about? I ask myself.

"How much have you raised for Bluerim so far?"

I remember reading that Bluerim is the name of a new hedge fund that Todd had launched earlier this year.

"With your contribution it is now well over three billion."

"And how safe?"

"Our similar 2007 hedge fund, UWM Distressed Mortgages, returned 29.5 percent last year."

"Not bad," Jorge replies.

"We can't expect to make what you make." Jorge raises his eyebrows. "But then we're legit," Todd ribs him. Both men laugh.

"We're just two businessmen doing our best to turn a profit," Jorge says as he prepares to leave. "Different kinds of business. Same corporate world."

"I'll have the paperwork ready for you on Monday," Todd says.

"Adiós, Todd. It's a deal," Jorge says as he makes for the door.

The recording switches off. I rewind it to the start of the conversation, but that consists of nothing more than greetings.

Jorge's voice is strangely familiar. It sounds identical to that of "Manuel," the guy who left a message on Susan's phone machine, offering to drop off a package from Todd.

He may also be the Jorge on the agreement at Total Surveillance. Why would a major private investor in Todd's funds want to bug his entire house? Doesn't Jorge trust him? After all, Todd's the CEO of the second-largest fund family in the US. Can this really have anything to do with Susan's disappearance?

I call Felicia.

"Hola?"

"Felicia. It's me, Jenny. I'm looking through those recordings from Todd's house."

"You mean the one from the kitchen?"

"It's not just the kitchen. Every major room in the house is being bugged."

"Dios mio! Why?"

"I wish I knew." I tell her about finding the tapes at Total Surveillance dating back to early August, commissioned by this guy called Jorge Valdez. After describing the taped conversation I heard between Todd and Jorge I ask Felicia whether she knows anything about him.

"Sí. Bad man. I've seen him at the house. I don't understand why Mr. Granger make business with a man like that."

"How often have you seen him at Todd's house?"

"Maybe twice. Mr. Granger, he meet him at the door each time and take him straight to the den. I bet he's a capo of some sort."

"A cartel boss?"

"Maybe a capo, maybe a lieutenant or something."

I consider this. "That would explain some of the things they said to one another on the recording."

"What's this to do with Susan?"

"I think the man who left the message on Susan's answering machine is Jorge. And the recordings start the day after Susan left Todd. Could that be a coincidence?"

"No lo entiendo. Is a mystery. But you clever, Jenny. You'll find the truth."

"You have more confidence in me than I do," I say. "I'll try. That's all I can promise."

There I go dissing myself again. Assuming I'll fail. Tricia has no difficulty overstating her business expertise to her clients. And it pays off. Why do I insist on minimizing mine? Am I protecting myself in case I fail? Or am I just trying to be honest?

*

I realize that I need to know more about Bluerim, the hedge fund into which Jorge was presumably depositing his billion dollars—A BILLION DOLLARS! One thousand million dollars! I can't begin to comprehend the size of that figure in the context of my own life. Let's see. Based on my pitiable current income of $30,000 a year, Jorge is depositing into Bluerim the equivalent of around 740 lifetimes of my income.

I do a Google search for Balboa Wealth Management Corporation and see that its customer assets have risen from a mere $200 million ten years ago to over a trillion dollars in 2010.

According to Bloomberg.com, in the last five years it has raised over $6 billion from institutional and individual private clients to buy up troubled mortgages and bonds backed by real estate loans that the government has forced banks to sell. Bluerim, a new private fund launched this year, is targeting smaller banks and lenders. A similar hedge fund launched last year made 29.5 percent in its first year (as Todd told Jorge).

Aren't all US funds supposed to declare their financial status and returns to the Securities and Exchange Commission? I go to the SEC's website. Surprise! It turns out that private hedge funds are exempt from the law requiring all other public funds to register and deliver prospectuses to all their shareholders. The SEC does have an online search system called EDGAR. When I enter "Bluerim" EDGAR shows that the corporation has filed what is called a Form D: Notice of Exempt Offering of Securities. The only information I can glean from this shining instance of nondisclosure is that Bluerim has already sold two billion dollars' worth of shares. But no clues as to whom it sold them. Another dead end.

What other leads are there? The only contact that I remember Susan mentioning was the director of the Coalition for Immigrant Rights. She used to do voluntary work for them once a week—

I hear the front door open and close, then Tricia getting something from the frig before turning on the living room TV. Chris Wallace, the host of Fox News Sunday, is talking about Dan Granger's bid to become Republican governor of California:

"To date, Granger has outspent Brown $173 million to $36.5 million. I predict another Republican will be keeping this left-leaning state in check for the next four years."

Another partisan panelist chimes in: "State Senator Granger has offered to take a polygraph test to prove that he was unaware that the construction worker he employed was illegal. Isn't that enough to dispose of this red herring and allow voters to concentrate on the real issue—the scandalous number of illegal workers living in California?"

Why does Tricia listen to this right-wing propaganda?

I abandon my online research and walk into the living room. Tricia is lounging in a trendy new chair in the shape of a cupped hand with colored digits providing the back and sides. Not my idea of comfort. We nod at one another.

She's sipping a glass of lemonade through a colored straw. On the screen Dan Granger addresses supporters at a rally: "My number one priority is jobs, jobs, jobs. Let's get rid of all the illegal workers and give their jobs to legitimate citizens."

"This," I remark, "from someone who employed an undocumented construction worker himself. What a hypocrite!"

"What do you expect?" Tricia snaps back. "He's a politician. Get real."

"If he wins, after he's thrown out all the undocumented workers he can find, half the fresh produce in the supermarkets will get too expensive for ordinary people like me to afford."

"So. Do something with your life."

"Like what?"

"Like taking a job that pays real money."

"That's your answer to everything."

"And what's yours? Socialism?"

"Socialism isn't a dirty word, you know."

"This is America, the greatest capitalist economy in the world. We believe in life, liberty, and the pursuit of happiness. That means each of us can pursue our idea of happiness without being forced to give up part of our income for slackers too lazy to work for a living."

"I thought we stood for taxes with representation," I say.

"Taxes! Look at the ridiculous ways the government spends our money. To hell with taxes."

"What about policemen or firefighters? What would you do without them?"

"Private security?"

"And for people who can't afford it?"

"Tough shit. Everyone needs to work for what they want. That's what America's about."

"It's also about justice—fairness for all."

"Do you know how much taxes I paid last year?"

"No. But I bet it was a lower percentage of your income than I paid."

"Typical! What a loser! Choose low-paid work and then complain about how little you earn."

"As usual, you're distorting what I'm saying. I was talking about unequal tax rates."

Tricia snatches up the remote and turns off the TV. "You live in an unreal world. No wonder this country's in such a mess, with supposedly intelligent people like you spouting garbage."

I remind myself that Tricia and I have covered this ground many times before, and it's never made a bit of difference. I change the subject. "So how did your evening work out?"

Tricia's shoulders drop. "Leap of Faith was fabulous. But Ralph drank so much sake at Kagaya, he slept through half of the show. When we got back to his place he switched to scotch. He passed out on me in the bedroom."

"Was that a happy escape for you? Or a letdown?"

"I needed to get laid. I thought we might get around to it in the morning, but he was already dressed in his biking outfit when I woke up. He belongs to some all-male bike club that puts in like fifty miles on Sunday mornings before stopping for breakfast . . . So I rang Rodney and we're taking his motor yacht out from the Marina to spend the rest of the day cruising down the coast."

"Sounds fantastic."

"It's really cool, like a floating condo with living room, bedroom, bathroom, every electronic device you could ever want, and an autopilot."

Tricia extricates herself from the upholstered fingers of her chair. "Got to get my sailing outfit together." She disappears into her bedroom.

Time for me to get moving. I phone the Coalition for Immigrants' Rights and ask to speak with the director. The receptionist informs me that his name is Eduardo Muñez. Surprise—I'm put straight through. After establishing my connection to Susan, I ask if I can come to his office to talk to him about her disappearance. He says that he too has been puzzled by her abrupt disappearance and that he'd like us to share what we know. I've just got time to make it there by 11:30, the time he suggests.

*

I'm rushing east on Olympic Boulevard in my trusty Corolla, to make the appointment. Actually, "trusty" isn't the most accurate descriptor; last time I brought my car in for service, the mechanic told me that all my tires were shot. I just didn't have an extra $250 to replace them, which leaves me constantly anxious while I'm driving, praying my tires won't explode on the freeway. So I tend to stick to the inner lane in case I need to make an emergency stop.

Sunday morning traffic is pleasurably light, and I'm listening to Pink's *Funhouse* album. The last number, "Sober," makes me think of Tricia. I'm not sure how deeply she was into drugs in high school.

I do know that to this day Tricia uses designer drugs when she is socializing, especially on weekends, but I don't know which drugs she uses, or how regularly she uses them, or where she gets them. Nursing a habit might account for her frequent bouts of depression.

Tricia and I have frank talks about our boyfriends, our parents, and our jobs, but they skim the surface of our lives. Despite sharing an apartment and a gene pool with Tricia, there's an awful lot I don't know about her. And the reverse is also true.

*

I enter the Coalition for Immigrants' Rights offices and ask the Latina receptionist for the director.

"You must be Ms. Carter," she says. "Please follow me."

We walk through a corridor lined with posters of Central American men and women performing various kinds of skilled work and crafts. In a sunlit office Eduardo rises from behind his paper-strewn desk and shakes my hand reassuringly. He probably offers the same feeling of reassurance to all his clients, most of whom likely badly need it.

Eduardo is decidedly handsome in an unassuming way, with a thick head of black wavy hair, a short-trimmed moustache, and a tanned face. He's wearing cream Levi's, a maroon shirt with the sleeves rolled up, and blue high tops with dark red laces.

"Ms. Carter. So you're a friend of Susan Kirby's." He waves me into a comfortable armchair. "Susan was a big help to us here. She used to come here for volunteer work almost every Wednesday. But we've not seen or heard from her for about three months now."

"That's what I came to talk to you about, Mr. Muñez."

"Please call me Eduardo."

"As long as you call me Jenny."

"Fair enough."

"You say you knew Susan through your employer?" he asks.

"That's right. She was his live-in girlfriend."

"'He' being Todd Granger?"

"Yes. Do you know him?"

"By repute. I know more about his brother who stands for everything I am fighting against."

"Yes, his campaign has been stoking fear of an immigrant takeover. What surprises me is that it is such a vote catcher. I can't stand him."

"You've spoken to him?

"At Todd's house, yes." I decide not to hold back. "He's a creep. He makes constant sexual innuendos. Snide comments. Leering looks when he thinks nobody's watching him. But he's too fixated on becoming the state's next governor to risk anything overt."

"Actually I'm hoping the Gomez incident might be enough to undermine his stance as an anti-immigration champion."

"Ah yes, Gomez, poor guy," I remark. "Shipped out of the country double quick."

"If only he'd got in touch with us." Eduardo sighs.

"To get back to Susan," I say, "Todd's housekeeper, Felicia, is so worried about her disappearance that she has asked me to try to trace her."

"Trace her?"

"Oh, I work part-time reviewing surveillance recordings at Total Surveillance. Felicia thinks that gives me magical powers to find Susan."

"Do you think Susan needs tracing?"

"She really does seem to have disappeared under strange circumstances." I tell him about Susan's moving out of Todd's house, her disappearance, her apartment in Palos Verdes, the strange rent checks, and the message on her voice mail.

Eduardo frowns. "It all sounds uncomfortably familiar."

"How do you mean?" I ask.

"If she were Latina I'd think she was mixed up with one of the cartels."

"Funny you say that. Felicia thought that the man who has had Todd's entire house bugged must be a leading member of a Mexican gang." I explain what I'd discovered by copying and playing back the SD cards.

"Who's the guy who commissioned the bugging?" Eduardo asks.

"Jorge Valdez."

Eduardo's eyes go big.

"Do you know him? Felicia thought he might be a capo."

Eduardo nods. "Not exactly a capo. But he is the brother of Pablo Valdez, the boss of the Baja Cartel. Look!" he says and points to a face on a Mexican government poster hanging on the wall behind him listing the country's ten most-wanted. "That's the brother."

"He looks like Jorge."

"Yes. Jorge is believed to be responsible for the Cartel's finances. Unlike his brother, he's clean as far as the law is concerned." Glancing at the poster Eduardo adds, "The Mexican government is offering a reward of thirty million pesos for Pablo Valdez's capture. That's more than two million dollars."

I've never paid much attention to Mexico's drug war. It never directly impacted my life. Now I am feeling embarrassingly uninformed. "And the Baja cartel smuggles drugs?"

"Drugs are their most profitable item. But I know about them because they also make millions of dollars smuggling Mexicans and Central Americans across the border."

"Is that so?" I say.

"They imprison the illegal immigrants in holding houses along the border until their families come up with a fee that's often more than their lifetime's savings. Once the immigrants are in the US, they frequently also demand a percentage of their wages here for years."

"Which side of the border are the safe houses on?" I want to know.

"Both." Eduardo gets up. "I can see this is all very new to you. Listen, Jenny, I'm starving. If you want me to fill you in more you're going to have to eat lunch with me. The restaurant's just around the corner."

"I didn't mean to take up so much of your time," I say to stop myself immediately accepting his offer, even though I'm dying to spend more time with him.

"Have you had lunch yet?"

"Nope," I respond.

"Then please join me."

"Well, thank you."

"Good. Let's go."

I feel mesmerized by Eduardo. He's so different. I'm happy for the opportunity to know him better.

*

Eduardo is obviously a regular at Paco's Grill. The genial host greets him by name and asks whether he wants his usual table on the patio.

"Sí, Hernandez. This is Señorita Jenny Carter. Ella es una private eye."

"Mucho gusto," Hernandez says. He shows us to our table in a secluded corner of the patio, prettily shielded from the midday sun by overhanging red bougainvillea. He hands us each a menu.

"Can I get you something to drink?" he asks me. "A margarita perhaps to keep you cool?"

"What are you drinking?" I ask Eduardo.

"Dos XX Amber, Hernandez, por favor."

"Naranjada, para mi." I tell him, flaunting my limited Spanish.

"I thought private eyes drank nothing but neat Scotch?" Eduardo teases me.

"They also spend an inordinate amount of their lives recovering from hangovers," I reply.

After a quick perusal of the menu, Eduardo orders chicken breast in mole poblano, and I order roast vegetable tacos with salsa verde and cilantro.

"So. The Baja Cartel," Eduardo begins, dipping a chip into the bowl of fiery salsa. "It used to be the largest narco-trafficking cartel in Mexico. It started on the west coast in the late 1960s and spread to seventeen Mexican states."

"Which drugs does the cartel sell?" I ask.

"Mostly Mexican marijuana, Colombian cocaine, Southeast Asian heroin and methamphetamine into the States. They're the ones who started digging tunnels underneath the border. They also use small planes and submarines."

"The Cartel's main rival is Los Zetas, a violent cartel that has recruited deserters from Mexico's elite security forces. The war between the two factions has badly cut into the Baja Cartel's profits, even though the Baja Cartel has penetrated not just the Mexican federal police and military, but deep into the Mexican government itself."

"Which puts the Mexican president on a par with Dan Granger," I remark.

Eduardo grins. "Now you're catching on." He pushes the basket of chips toward me. "Please dig into the chips before I eat all of them," he urges me.

"Thanks." I take a couple and push the basket back.

"This corruption has been going on for decades," Eduardo continues. "It started long before Calderón began his phony war on the drug cartels. But now, to compensate for their recent downturn in drug profits, the Baja Cartel has taken to kidnapping and smuggling illegals from all over Central and South America. That is, besides stealing oil from Mexican pipelines. They have commandeered most of the operations of the previously independent coyotes and turned this into a multibillion-dollar-a-year business. The Baja Cartel is even stealing truckloads of 'chickens'—as they call their human cargo—from their rivals. Then they charge the immigrants a second fee, which often can only be paid back through prostitution or forced labor—up to $4,500 for getting them to the US and providing them with fake papers."

"Where do the immigrants get that kind of money?" I ask.

"Family savings. Mortgaging the family house. Selling the family car." Eduardo shrugs at me. "Human smuggling is their major revenue source between the two marijuana-growing seasons. They grossed two billion from it last year. The cost is high. Seven thousand people died last year in the war between the cartels."

"How horrible," I say.

"American politicians play on the fear that the same kind of violence will break out here—unless we ship out the illegal aliens, all of whom belong to the cartels in the politicians' minds. You can see these gangsters bent over double in strawberry fields all over the state plotting their next attack."

We grin at each other as our lunches are delivered. The spicy hot aroma rising from the plates awakes my appetite.

"Which brings us back," I say, "to Dan Granger."

Eduardo's face contorts with anger. "Jenny, now you're turning my pechuga de pollo sour with the mention of that lying bastard."

Considering Eduardo's life's work, he has every reason to be angry at Dan for his fearmongering lies. His passion warms me. Is that because I've grown so tired of Gary's lack of emotion? Or my own?

Our instant empathy makes me feel I can trust him with information I would normally withhold from someone I'd just met.

"I share your feelings about him. I despise what he stands for, and I also despise him as an individual," I say.

"You would despise him even more if you knew what I recently learned."

"And what is that?"

"This is confidential, Jenny. But I believe I can trust you, and it might help you in your own search."

"Now I'm really interested."

Eduardo leans forward and lowers his voice. "Two weeks ago I was contacted by a disgruntled staffer in Dan Granger's campaign team. Let's call him Steve. Steve told me that Dan Granger had had lunch with Jorge Valdez earlier this week. Steve knew who Valdez was because he used to work for the DEA. He was outraged that Granger would have dealings with a member of the Cartel. Two days later Dan Granger told Steve to open a personal checking account under a pseudonym so that he could deposit in it a check from Dan's brother. That's when Steve quit."

"That's unbelievable."

"I was skeptical myself. But he showed me the bank's confirmation of the new account. It was opened under the name of David Smithson. Clearly an illegal campaign contribution"

I lean in close, pushing my plate aside. "On my job I saw a video of Jorge arranging to invest a billion dollars in one of Todd's hedge funds."

"Which one?"

"Bluerim. It's a new private equity fund you might not have heard of."

"I haven't," says Eduardo with growing respect for my inside information.

"On the recording Todd also mentioned the sum of $100,000 as an extra payment. Admittedly that doesn't definitively connect Valdez to Dan Granger."

"No. It doesn't. But the sum coincides with a figure Dan mentioned to Steve."

"What I don't understand," I say, "is why a cartel that depends on smuggling immigrants into this country would want to give money to a candidate for governor who's campaigning on an anti-immigrant ticket."

"That's not so hard to figure. If the state adopts new stricter anti-immigration measures under a Republican governor, the cartels can charge more to bring immigrants across the border."

"In politics nothing is what it seems, it seems."

He smiles. "And no one says what he means."

Eduardo asks for the check and waves aside my credit card.

It's uncanny. He seems to be on exactly the same wavelength as me. I feel as if we've known each other for years. And all my senses are working overtime. With the first bite of my tacos I could taste every separate ingredient in the salsa—the tomatillos, red onion, cilantro, and chili. The bougainvillea throbs blood-red above me. In the background the strains of musica norteña seem to be playing inside my head. I'm on sensory overload.

"Really, Jenny, I haven't had such an enjoyable lunch for ages," Eduardo says, getting up.

"I enjoyed it, too. Thank you so much, Eduardo—for the meal and for all the helpful information." I want to say so much more, but I don't dare.

"Please get in touch if there's anything else I can help you with," Eduardo says as we take our leave.

We stare into each other's eyes. We've finally run out of any reasons to prolong our time together. I reach out to shake his hand. Instead Eduardo kisses me lightly on the cheek. Its trace of moisture lingers tingling as it slowly evaporates on my skin long after I return to my car and hit the road once more.

*

Back at the apartment mid-afternoon, I'm feeling at once elated and flat. Why couldn't my lunch with Eduardo go on forever? How very different he is from Gary—outgoing, passionately engaged, socially committed. What was it that kept me seeing Gary for how many years?—was it seven? Good God!

Maybe Tricia's constant put-downs of Gary brought out the stubborn streak in me and made me perversely refuse to see his many faults. I know I also tend to avoid taking risks. How ridiculous that I threw away so many years, those irreplaceable years in my twenties, out of sheer obstinacy.

I still have three years before I turn thirty. What do I want to do with them? What do I want to do with the rest of my life? I know this: I don't want to waste any more of it on dead-end jobs and dead-end boyfriends. Life, I'm coming to realize, is not just what happens to you. It is what you make happen.

I settle onto the couch, attempting to calm myself by watching TV. Instead I find the obnoxious Dan Granger addressing a crowd of Republican businesswomen.

". . . we're all investors in California. We all have an interest in how well it performs. But for the past ten years or more the unions have controlled Sacramento. They're driving away innovation, driving away business, because now the state has some of the highest taxes in the country to pay for the unions' grossly inflated pensions and health benefits."

This leads me to reflect that, although I don't have an employee pension and can't afford health benefits, I'm paying through my taxes for these benefits for others.

So this is how it works. Granger is making me feel resentful because others are being offered what all of us should be offered. I have always believed that we should all qualify for a pension and affordable health insurance.

I try flipping through the channels, but I'm drawn back to the coverage of the governor's race. A crowd of demonstrators outside the hotel where Granger's speaking is circling the hotel entrance, chanting, "Granger, go home!"

"Dan Granger began his address to a crowd estimated at 6,000 by downing a shot of tequila," says the news commentator. "He has been targeting Spanish-speaking voters by inundating Latino channels with political advertisements promising immigrants a path to citizenship. Yet in the primaries he accused his Republican rival of offering them an amnesty, and on English-speaking stations he swears that as governor he would prosecute employers found employing illegal aliens. The latest poll, taken after news broke that Granger has employed an undocumented immigrant, shows him trailing Brown by thirty points among Latino voters."

I've heard all this before. I turn off the TV and open my laptop, eager to complete my review of the discs from Todd's house.

The third card I fast-forward through is from the dining room. I watch Felicia serving Todd and Dan bowls of soup. I switch the recording to PLAY as Felicia leaves the room.

Todd: "Felicia's gazpacho is unique. I hope you have a strong stomach."

Dan: "You know me of old. I love the hottest chilies. It's worth the brief moment of pain for the rush of pleasure. It's like taking crack."

Todd "Of course, you'd know all about that."

Dan: "Actually I prefer cocaine mixed with K."

Todd: "Because?"

Dan: "Because cocaine is an upper while K relaxes you. Great combination. And you?"

Todd: "Still an abstainer."

Dan: "Your loss."

Todd: "Or gain."

Dan: "You always did have exceptional self-control."

Todd: "And you always had a flair for self-dramatizing."

Dan: "That's why I'm in politics and you're in the investment business. I'm much too impulsive to run a mutual fund."

Todd: "And I'm too cautious—and private—to throw myself into the rough-and-tumble of politics."

Dan: "Which is why together we can make anything happen."

They fall silent as Felicia reenters, clears their soup bowls, places a plate in front of each of them, and leaves three dishes of food on the table.

Todd: "Which reminds me: Jorge is wiring me your $100,000 Monday morning."

Dan: "Great! That should just about bring my campaign budget back from the red."

[So that was what the $100,000 was for, I think.]

Todd: "Now all you've got to do is win the election."

Dan: "Damn Gomez. He would have to go and fall off the scaffolding just weeks before Election Day."

Todd: "Couldn't you have bought him off?"

Dan: "If only. The press caught wind of the accident before I could get to him."

Todd: "It has certainly been a setback. But you've got a huge advantage in spending."

Dan: "Yep. However, I'm still down a small margin in our private polls, Ron tells me. He reckons I have a small lead among independents, thanks to my stance on undocumented workers. We'll see."

So. There's the missing link between Dan Granger and the Cartel. And I have the hard evidence. I make a second copy for safety's sake— and because I want to give Eduardo a copy, which will make a great excuse for reconnecting with him.

*

I'm on a high, reliving every moment of my lunch with Eduardo and the way we connected instantly.

Does he feel the same way? Or is he just a polite guy who would have been as engaged with whomever he happened to be having lunch with?

But what if he's married or already has a girlfriend? I decide to google him. Entries with his name fill the screen. But none of the links I try says anything about his personal life.

I decide to treat myself by baking a quiche lorraine, using turkey bacon, leeks, low fat Gruyère, and milk rather than cream in deference to my health. When the timer goes off I lift the golden-brown tart from the oven shelf and place it on a stainless-steel rack.

While waiting for it to cool I pour myself a glass of Tricia's expensive Brunello red wine and set up Beyoncé's "Single Ladies" to play on the iPod dock. The song is just ending with, "If you liked it you should have put a ring on it" when Tricia gets home from her day on the ocean.

"I'm so glad Dreary didn't want to put a ring on it," she comments, dropping a designer shopping bag full of her new acquisitions on the rug.

"You know what? So am I," I surprise myself by saying.

"I see you are enjoying my Brunello."

"I'm kind of celebrating. Can I pour you a glass?" the new me responds unapologetically.

"Why not, since I went out specially for it yesterday."

Ignoring her sarcasm, I pour a glass and hand it to her.

"It's definitely worth the effort," I say. "One of the world's great reds."

"What smells so good?" she asks.

"I made a quiche lorraine," I announce. "Want some?"

"I suppose you used up all the eggs?"

"It only takes four. You've still got two left."

"Well, thanks for that small mercy," she says bad-temperedly.

"Your trip not work out as you expected?" I ask.

"Guys! What can I say? Rodney turns out to be a bit kinky. He only likes to do it from the rear."

"So?"

"I mean literally up my rear. As I said to him, how's that supposed to make me come? But he was too into it to pay me much attention. So the day was not a roaring success."

"I'm sorry."

"Your pity is the last thing I need," Tricia replies with irritation.

"How about a slice of quiche and some salad?" I ask to calm her down.

"Great. Let's have it here on the coffee table. And please turn Beyoncé off. She's giving me an inferiority complex."

I turn off the music, add more greens to the salad, dress it, and cut two slices of quiche for us.

"Help yourself to salad," I say.

Tricia takes a bite of quiche. "You always were a better cook than me. Do you remember that amazing chocolate and raspberry cake you baked for Dad and Mom's anniversary that time?"—

How could I forget? I was sixteen. I made it as a surprise. I wanted to bring it out with candles blazing just when Mom was about to serve up dessert. Tricia was late getting home, and I was forced to stage my dramatic entry on my own. They were both oohing and aahing when the front door crashed open and Tricia staggered into the dining room clearly smashed out of her mind.

"How touching!" she sneered. "Playing happy families?"

"Tricia," Dad said, "that's enough. Sit down and have some cake with us."

"Not unless you want me to throw up."

"Have you forgotten that your mother and I planned to celebrate our thirtieth anniversary today with the two of you?"

"I'm here, aren't I?" she blurted out, collapsing onto a dining room chair.

"If you remember, the idea was for all of us to share a special dinner here—*together*. Your mother went to a lot of trouble preparing stuffed game hens for us."

"I hate game hens. Please don't talk to me any more about food or I'll definitely throw up."

"Where have you been to get yourself into this state?" Dad asked.

"I went home with some friends to Glenda's house after school." She let out a loud burp. "Her parents were out, and she threw a spontaneous party. Harry made a lethal sangria for us. He had no idea how much brandy to add, and we all got plastered. Don't blame me. I planned on being back here long before now."

"Who else should we blame?" Dad asked.

"Did you hear a word I just said?" Tricia shocked us all with her aggressiveness.

"That is no way to speak to your father" Mom said.

"What do you want me to do? Call him 'Sir'?"

"That will be enough, Tricia," Mom said sharply.

"I'm not a child. I can say what I like."

"No one can just say what they like in this world," Mom replied.

"Now we're going to dispense words of adult wisdom," Tricia sneered.

"That's enough for tonight, do you hear?" Dad said firmly.

"Excuse me. I think I'm about to upchuck," Tricia exclaimed, and she rushed out to the bathroom from where ugly sounds of choking, retching, and coughing confirmed her diagnosis all too vividly.

Mom lost it and broke out sobbing, dripping tears onto her slice of cake. Dad said I could go to bed. I left apologizing for Tricia—of all things.

Thinking back on it I can understand that our parents' excessive reasonableness must have made Tricia overreact. How else could she assert herself?

"Yes, Tricia. I sure as hell remember."

"After Mom and Dad had gone to bed that evening," Tricia says, "I sneaked down and sampled your cake. Sick in my stomach as I was feeling, I still remember how delicious it was."

"Mom threw it out next day. It was too painful a reminder."

"And how did that make you feel?"

"Hurt. Conflicted."

"But you never said anything to her?"

"I suppose I should have. But you know me. I always opt for peace and harmony."

"And where has that got you? Years of Dreary. Years of long hours at minimum pay. Wake up, Jenny. The world's out there waiting for you. All you have to do is take what you want."

"If only I knew what I want. Besides, I believe in giving as well as taking."

"I can't believe you want what you currently have."

"I don't. But I don't have a clear idea of what I want to do with my life, the way you do. I want more than just heaps of dollars."

"So do I. But you can only get what you want if you have the money to buy it."

As I'm about to disagree with her, my phone rings. It's Felicia on the line.

"Jenny," Felicia says. "Is terrible."

"What's the matter, Felicia?"

"Miguel just called me. From jail."

"Why is he in jail?"

"La Migra got him. They are deporting him."

"They can't just do that. There has to be a hearing before a judge."

"No hearing. He signed papers."

"What papers?"

"Papers that say he don't want a hearing."

"He waived his rights? Why would he do that?"

"They threaten him. Tell him he had to stay in detention center for months, years. He say he don't want to do that. So he sign the papers. They deport him fast. I don't know what to do. His mother cry all the time on the phone. She says they cannot help him because the migra comes after them. What do I do? Is terrible."

"I have an idea," I say. "I could speak to my new friend, Eduardo. He's the director of the Coalition for Immigrants' Rights." My heart leaps at the thought of seeing Eduardo again. I'm ashamed at feeling this when Felicia is so distraught. "Susan used to work as a volunteer for him, remember?"

"Sí. I remember she talked about him. Said he was simpatico."

"I went to see him today about Susan. So I can ask him whether there is something we can do."

"Please, Jenny. I feel so bad for his family."

"Leave it with me. I'll call you after I've talked to Eduardo."

"Muchísimas gracias."

I turn back to Tricia. "Hell! Felicia's nephew has been arrested as an illegal and has signed his rights away."

"Don't expect me to sympathize. You know how I feel about illegal aliens."

"Miguel isn't a being from outer space. He's lived here almost all his life."

She shrugs. "But he wasn't born here. Right?"

"What are you saying? That he doesn't have a right to be here?"

She shrugs her shoulders.

"I have to do something to help."

"Always the enabler, even if you get nothing for it."

"How about friendship? How about human sympathy? —"

"You've always been good at justifying doing something for nothing."

"I've got to make a call," I say. Suspending our never-ending argument, I make for my bedroom.

*

Slumped on my bed with Lulu purring next to me, I dial Eduardo's cell phone.

"Bueno? Diga."

"Eduardo?"

"Sí. Quién habla?"

"It's me. Jenny."

"Oh, Jenny. How nice to hear your voice."

"Nice to hear yours," I say. "Do you remember I mentioned that Todd's housekeeper, Felicia, has a nephew she worries about?"

"Yes."

"Well, Miguel wasn't born here, which is why she worries about him. And today he got picked up by ICE agents and taken downtown."

"We can certainly assign a lawyer to his case."

"The problem is Miguel signed away his rights and agreed to a fast-track deportation."

"Oh, no! This is ICE's favorite move recently. It's called stipulated removal. At the rate they're going the government will have deported over 35,000 illegal aliens this year using that loophole. And the problem is that anyone deported with a stipulated removal order is barred from reentering the country for ten years."

"It doesn't sound good for him."

"It isn't." Eduardo says. "We can try to locate Miguel before they send him across the border, but he could be in any of a number of detention facilities. Or he could be in the process of being moved from one to another."

"Isn't he allowed to make a call, to let someone know where he is?"

"In theory he is. But there's always a shortage of detainee phones. And often they only allow a detainee his phone call hours before deporting him."

"It makes me feel ashamed of the government I voted in two years ago."

"Don't get me started on the Obama administration's immigration policies."

"McCain would almost certainly have been worse."

"True."

"Is there anything we can do for Miguel?" I ask.

"First, we have to locate him. Then we can see whether we can appeal his case on the grounds that ICE didn't inform him fully of his rights. I tell you what. Can you come to my office tomorrow at 9, when the detention facilities open? Then we can call the locations where he is likely being held."

"Sure." I realize that I don't really have to be there in person. Maybe he wants what I want: an excuse to be together.

"Great," he says. "Until tomorrow morning, then."

I roll onto my back and conjure up a picture of us in his office, surreptitiously checking each other out as we make our calls.

*

Right after Eduardo on my to-do list is my dad, and his plan to hijack my mother to Oklahoma. I call him and make a date to meet him for coffee at a hip spot on Ventura. I park easily for a change, probably because it's early Sunday evening.

I find Dad sitting at an outdoor table under an orange awning, looking uncomfortable, surrounded by groups of kids less than a third his age peering at their phones and tablets. I greet him with a hug and a kiss on the cheek and ask him what he'd like to drink.

"A macchiato," he says.

"How do you know what a macchiato is?" I say before I can stop myself.

"I may be old, Jenny. I'm not dead," he answers.

"And a pastry?"

"No, thanks," he replies, rubbing his hand over his protruding stomach by way of explanation.

I enter the café's dark interior where customers' shouted conversations and heavy metal music on the speakers ricochet between the bare bricked walls and exposed ceiling conduits, while the wall-mounted TV silently flickers light on several blackboards on which the large menu is handwritten in colored chalk. I order Dad's coffee, a hot chai tea latte for myself, and one of their famous crepes filled with strawberries, Nutella, and cream. Dad, I know, will steal some of it.

I return to Dad, bearing napkins, tableware, and a table number in a tall chrome holder.

"See that motorbike cop?" Dad greets me. "He's been writing tickets nonstop ever since I sat down here. The last one was for not wearing a seat belt."

I take in the cop, the car, and its occupants.

"It only shows how desperate the city is for revenue," I remark.

"I know. I know. But I wish he didn't seem to enjoy his job so much."

"You don't know that, Dad."

"I don't understand where you and Tricia got your ideas from. Your mother and I always taught you to distrust authority of any kind. It's just an instrument of state terror."

"You're right, Dad," I humor him. "But demonstrations and political protests seem so pointless today."

This only gets him fired up again. "That's the trouble with your generation," he sputters. "You leave it to corporations and politicians to decide things for you. The nearest you get to protesting anything is signing online petitions." He pauses. "And your sister probably doesn't even do that."

"That's not fair, Dad. Young people got Obama elected in 2008."

"If McCain had won I think I would have emigrated to another country."

"That reminds me. Mom tells me that you're thinking of taking a job in Oklahoma, of all places."

"True," he concedes.

"Why on earth do you want to live in the Bible Belt? You know Oklahoma has voted Republican since 1964. McCain got two-thirds of the Oklahoma vote in 2008."

"More reason to move there and start changing that."

"And what about Mom? How's she going to adapt to a strange new place? All her friends live here in the Valley."

"You haven't spent much time with your mother lately, have you?"

I'm about to get defensive, but Dad interrupts me: "I'm not complaining about that. You and Tricia have your own lives to live. But over the last year Mom's been acting very strangely." So Dad's noticing what I've been noticing recently about Mom.

"How?" I ask.

"She won't leave the house except for work and shopping."

"Why is that, do you think?"

"Our doctor told me she's suffering from acute depression."

"Oh, no. I'm so sorry. Did the doc put her on meds?"

"He prescribed antidepressants. Big surprise."

"You sound depressed yourself, Dad."

"That's because the drugs seem to make her symptoms worse. She's blaming me for the way she feels."

"Do you think you're to blame in any way?"

My crepe and Dad's coffee arrive. Dad eyes my plate, as I knew he would; so I cut him a sizable slice and fetch him a plastic knife and fork to eat it with.

I am about to repeat my question when he blurts out, "I wish I could say that I'm to blame."

"What does she blame you for?"

"You name it. Her hard life. Her repetitive routine. The drudgery of running our home. Even her shrinking circle of friends."

"Why is she losing friends?"

"Because she's constantly complaining about her life and making them feel guilty and miserable for anything good about their lives."

"Have you thought of taking her in for a second opinion?"

"You bet I have. But she refuses to accept that there's anything wrong with her. She says it's all my fault."

This is the first I've heard of my mother venting anger at my father. "Does she give a reason?"

"She says it's because I've dedicated my working life to a low-paying social service job that won't support us when we retire."

"Will it?"

"I qualify for a decent pension, which at least partly compensates for my crappy salary. But now they're talking about cutting back our pensions. It makes me start to wonder whether she isn't right. I've spent my life trying to make America a little fairer, and now they're telling me they can't afford to pay for my retirement."

Dad sighs. "Just to make myself feel a little better, I'm stealing another mouthful of your crepe."

"Go ahead. You've just killed my appetite."

"It's our problem, dear. You've got your own, I'm sure. Your mother tells me you and Gary broke up"

I ignore this. "How does Mom's state of mind relate to your plan to move to Oklahoma?"

"I thought the adventure of moving might distract her. But it's only made her more angry at me. She's accusing me of trying to take her away from the only friends she has."

"Isn't that true?"

"She hasn't got any friends left. They all avoid her these days."

"Oh, dear."

"Which is why I'm turning down the offer."

"You're turning it down?"

"That's right. We're not moving."

"What? Then why did Mom just tell me you were?"

"I only decided just now as we were talking."

At this moment Dad's attention is caught by the Anglo cop who's just pulled over a young African American woman driver of a beat-up old Chevy. After pointing out a missing taillight and asking for her license and insurance, which she produces, he tells all three young occupants of the car to step out and put their hands on the roof.

"What's wrong with him?" Dad asks in a booming voice. "So her taillight's out. Write her a ticket. What's the big deal?"

The cop overhears Dad, as he intended him to. He struts over to our table. "I should warn you, sir," he says, "that obstructing a police officer in the course of his duty is a criminal offense. If you have anything you want to say to me I suggest you wait until I have dealt with this matter."

Dad isn't that easily cowed. "I noticed, Officer, that you let all those earlier traffic offenders stay in their cars while you wrote them tickets. But the first time you pull over an African American driver you have to treat her and her passengers like dangerous criminals."

"Sir. Last warning. I suggest you butt out of my business."

"As a citizen who pays your salary, I have a right to question how you conduct yourself."

"Not if you are interfering with me doing my duty." The cop's voice is now threatening. "Are we done?"

"Yes, we're done," I interject, turning to Dad. "I have to go," I lie to him. "I'll walk with you to your car."

Dad looks baffled. I shake my head and lead him to his car. We part as we greeted one another, with a kiss and a hug.

On the walk back to my car I realize I'm shaking from the confrontation with the cop. Dad, however, had remained unfazed. He may be a liberal, but he has the same fire that Tricia shows.

*

Back at the apartment, I find Tricia lounging in her hand-shaped chair, holding a glass of whiskey up to the light.

"This is the closest you can get to drinking liquid gold," she announces without looking up, slurring her words. She must have had a lot to drink; Tricia can hold her liquor better than anyone else I know.

"What've you been up to?" I ask.

"I went to hear Narcoleptic Youth play at a pop-up in North Hollywood."

"And how were they?"

"They're a good Californian punk band. But they got into a confrontation with their fans for taking videos of them on their phones. When the fans started booing and catcalling, the band stopped in mid-song and walked off stage. So—not a memorable evening."

That reminds me of one evening when Tricia insisted I come with her and her boyfriend of the time to a performance of a band I'd never heard of. I must have been sixteen. It was all very secretive. The three of us drove to a gas station where we were greeted by three ugly-looking guys with shaved heads and gross tattoos. They asked Mike, Tricia's boyfriend, a number of questions, all of which seemed racially charged, like, "D'you see yourself as an Aryan?" and "Own any Resistance Records albums?" and "What power bands have you heard

118

previously?" Mike readily responded in their jargon. Satisfied, they told him where to drive for the event.

All this rigmarole scared me. The site for the performance turned out to be an unused warehouse in the Valley, with a wooden platform supported by bare scaffolding for stage. The band was already playing and the fans careening around when we arrived. "EXTREME HATE," the name of the band, was hand painted in red on a black banner hung carelessly over the makeshift stage. The players, all heavyset skinheads, wore swastika armbands and ghoulish facial makeup. The music was incredibly loud, repetitive, and badly played. Mike called it "hatecore rock." The crowd had formed a large circle close to the stage. Those inside it were flailing their arms and legs in aggressive fashion, often hitting one another.

I began to hear snatches of the lyrics being bawled out by the band: "stand up and fight," "had it up to here," "raise the white man's flag," "just killed a kike," "overrun by queers"!

If I'd had my own transport I would have been out of there in five minutes. Instead I had to watch Mike leap into the mosh pit, as he called it, whirling round in small circles while flailing his arms inches from the surrounding watchers. Suddenly, one of the watchers was pushed out into his path and was hit hard in the eye by his hand. To my amazement Mike put his hand on the guy's shoulder; his victim grinned and rejoined the melee as he held one hand over what was likely to turn into a black eye. Clearly to them this was good clean fun. By the time Mike left the circle he had a trickle of blood dribbling from the side of his mouth and was limping from a bruised knee. By then I was half deaf from the cacophonous music. I was also frightened by the violence that seemed to energize everyone else and threatened to suck us into its orbit any moment.

Tricia seemed totally unmoved by the mixture of rage, hate, and fear driving everyone. It turned her on, if anything. She cleaned Mike's face off with a tissue and gave him a long open-mouthed kiss.

When I asked her later whether she realized what all the hate songs were about, she shrugged me off with, "It takes all kinds . . ." Without a pause she then asked me, "Don't you think Mike's really sexy?"

"I think he's pathetic," I replied, "with his hang-ups about nonwhites and his fantasies about fighting."

"You should see him naked, and you'd find it hard to think that," was all she said.

Was my older sister a racist? I asked myself. Rather, I told myself, in reacting against our parents Tricia seemed to have given up on ethics of all kinds. Within weeks she had stopped seeing Mike. But not because of his rabid opinions.

I wish her goodnight and fall into bed, exhausted.

MIGUEL

After being driven to ICE's Los Angeles Field Office downtown, Miguel is "processed," which means he is strip-searched, his wallet with his money and documentation confiscated, and then fingerprinted, photographed, and placed in a holding cell by himself. He remains there with no food or drink—just a bucket for a toilet with no toilet paper. Why couldn't he have kept his big mouth shut? he asks himself. But another voice asks, how else could he keep his self-respect? Unprovoked, the agent was abusing that poor, frightened girl in front of them all. He simply said what everyone was thinking.

Suddenly the cell door is unlocked. A guard gestures for Miguel to follow him out of his cell and into a room where an official wearing a navy sweatshirt with POLICE ICE in huge white block letters waves him to a chair facing his desk. The official has a shaved head, flaring nostrils, a double chin, and drooping jowls. His manner is impassive, robot-like.

"Name?" he barks.

"Miguel Mondragon."

"Social security number?"

Miguel recites the number.

"Are you aware that that number matches that of a man in Pensacola, Florida, who died in 1998?"

Miguel shrugs. "There is some mistake."

"Don't bullshit me." Raising his voice, the agent glares at him.

Miguel says nothing.

"You and I both know that you're an undocumented alien."

The term sounds so formal to Miguel. "Wetback," or "Floater," he's used to. The legal term sounds much more threatening.

"I spent my entire life here in America." Miguel says calmly. "My first and only language is English. I graduated from West Covina High School. I work at—"

"Now you're bullshitting me some more. If you were born here you'd have a legitimate social security number of your own."

Miguel clams up. He was brought to the States by his parents when he was just one-and-a-half. He has no memory of his first eighteen months in Mexico.

"Where do you live?"

"West Covina."

"Address?"

Miguel hesitates. He isn't going to give La Migra information that would enable them to arrest the rest of his family. He stays silent.

"I said, what is your address?"

"I know my rights. I don't have to say anything I don't want to."

The agent raises his voice threateningly. "Rights! You have no rights. You are in this country illegally."

Miguel shrugs. "I am still not giving you my address." He waits for the storm to break.

Instead the agent addresses him as one reasonable human being to another. "Listen here, Miguel. There's a choice you need to make. You can waste my time and everyone else's time by continuing to deny the obvious—that you're here illegally. If you continue to insist on this obvious lie you'll spend six months to three years in a detention center waiting for the inevitable—deportation. You know what life in a detention center is like?"

Miguel shakes his head, though a friend of his did describe his experience of one last year, and it sounded terrible.

"Shall we say extremely uncomfortable? And the end result will be the same—a forced trip over the border."

"So what other choice do I have?" Miguel asks.

"What's called a fast-track deportation, which would mean that you would be released over the border in a matter of days."

"It's so unfair," Miguel says. "I've been here my whole life. I've never broken the law—"

"I know that," interrupts the agent. "We've checked your records, and they're clean."

"I contributed to the economy and paid my taxes. It's just not fair."

"I don't make the laws. I simply enforce them. Legally, you have no defense."

Miguel stays silent.

"So why sentence yourself to months of unpleasant confinement?"

Miguel sees the sense in his argument. Why put off the inevitable and make his life a nightmare? On the other hand, what alternative options might be open to him? If only he had more time to think things through.

"What do I have to do?" he asks.

"Just sign these papers." The agent pushes a set of official documents across the desk. Miguel looks at the stack. Emerging from the sides are Post-it arrows indicating where Miguel's signature should go.

The top page is headed:

STIPULATED REQUEST FOR REMOVAL ORDER AND WAIVER OF HEARING.

"What does this mean?" Miguel asks, pointing to the first sentence. "'I have received a legal aid list.'"

"Just a formality," the agent replies reassuringly. "But here's a copy if that makes you feel better."

He hands Miguel a printed list of immigration lawyers in the city.

Faced with so many technical terms, Miguel feels out of his depth. He tries to remain calm.

"And what are the 'allegations in the NTA' that I have admitted to?" Miguel asks uncertainly.

"Notice To Appear," the agent replies. "That's what you're waiving your rights to."

"Appear where?" Miguel persists.

"Before an immigration judge." The agent's getting more annoyed with each question.

"And what do I admit?" If only he had time to think clearly, Miguel thinks.

"THE OBVIOUS!" the agent snaps with obvious annoyance. "That you're in the US with false documentation. Any more stupid questions?"

Miguel feels dizzy. He can't think straight.

"But I don't admit that my papers are false."

"You don't have to, idiot. They're false whether you say so or not."

Miguel feels his grip on the situation slip away. It all seems so hopeless. However unjust it is, he has no legal case. His social security number is fraudulent. What can he do?

"I'll sign," he blurts out.

"Then do it—here, and here, and here."

Miguel's head feels like it's going to burst. He just can't see a better option. Defeated, he signs his name again and again and again.

NOVEMBER 1, 2010

I listen to Rihanna all the way to Eduardo's mid-Wilshire office, singing along to her sexy fantasies, while reminding myself that I've only met Eduardo in person once. For all I know he's already in a relationship. Or gay. Or just not interested in me. Still, my heart is racing as Sofia, his assistant, leads me down the hall. How many hopeful, smitten women has she led to Eduardo's office, I wonder.

Eduardo greets me with a warm hug. He shows me to a comfortable chair next to a low coffee table.

"Coffee?" he asks me before Sofia leaves the room.

"Already had too much, thanks," I reply.

"I probably have too." He turns to Sofia. "One coffee then, please."

"One of my vices," he grins at me. "Caffeine only, for breakfast."

"If that's a vice, the whole country's in trouble."

"It's not my worst vice, though," he adds. Am I dreaming, or is he flirting with me?

"I won't ask you what that is," I flirt back, just in case.

"Of course, being a woman, you have no vices," he teases.

"Rest assured. I have more than my share."

"What a relief," Eduardo says, and we both laugh.

Eduardo pulls out a sheet of notepaper.

"As there are only a small number of detention centers in California, I have decided to make all the calls myself."

I was hoping for more flirting first. I remind myself that he's doing me a big favor, helping me do something I wouldn't even know how to start doing on my own. I am feeling confused—grateful and disappointed at the same time.

"What's Miguel's full name?" Eduardo asks.

"Miguel Mondragon."

"Good. Here goes."

I listen to him go through the routine with the first center, in Santa Ana. It only takes us about twenty minutes to get through the list. The officials at the end of the line are uniformly curt and negative. Miguel has disappeared into the system. Or the system's records haven't caught up with his movements. He has become what he was charged with being—stateless, a non-being.

"Don't be frustrated," Eduardo reassures me. "This often happens when a detainee is in transit. We'll try again later in the day."

"You've already done enough," I say without conviction. "I can take the list with me and call again this afternoon." I can't believe I just suggested this.

Happily, he rejects my offer. "What will you do if a center confirms that they're holding him?"

"Phone you," I say sheepishly.

"So what's the point? I'll try all of the centers again later and let you know as soon as I have located him."

I reflect how superfluous I have been. That suggests that he was looking for an excuse to see me again. Which makes me feel good.

"I don't know how to thank you," I say.

"I can think of a few ways," Eduardo says, laughing.

I look at him with my eyebrows raised.

"Just joking," he says.

Don't be just joking, I implore him silently. "Seriously," I say. "I owe you one."

"Are you going to give me an IOU?"

"You've already got it."

"Sounds interesting," Eduardo says.

He walks me down the hall to the front door. We turn to one another to say goodbye. Impulsively I pull his head down with both hands and kiss him briefly on each cheek. Then I make a hurried exit, mortified by my pushiness.

*

I have hardly got back to the apartment when my phone rings.

"Hello, Jenny." It's Dad.

"Hi, Dad. What's up?" I ask.

"I'm not sure whether I should be sharing this with you."

"Sharing what?"

"What happened when I got home last night."

"Tell me, Dad."

"I found your mother sitting at the kitchen table staring at a pile of antidepressants she had poured out in a heap—at least two weeks' worth."

"You mean she was planning on taking them all?" I'm in shock.

"When I think back on it now, I don't know whether she staged this for me, or whether I had interrupted her from swallowing them all."

"Even if it was only meant as a warning shot, this needs to be taken seriously."

"I know that. When I saw her like that I broke down crying. I couldn't even say anything for ten minutes."

"I'm sorry, Dad. What happened next?"

"I told her we couldn't go on like this. Either we got a second opinion, or I would have to move out."

"Very likely! I doubt whether she believed that threat for a moment," I say.

His reply surprises me. "She responded, 'Typical! You just needed a good excuse to abandon me by going to Oklahoma—and ruin my life in the process.'"

"She sounds very bitter."

"When I told her that I had decided not to take the job there, she just got angrier. She shot back, 'And you think that will make me feel any better? At least there I could have made new friends.'"

"Oh, dear," I sigh. "She seems to want it both ways. That suggests that she's really confused."

"I tried again. 'I beg you,' I pleaded, 'please let me make you an appointment with a psychiatrist.' She stormed out of the room."

"Poor Dad. Is there anything I can do?"

"I'm not asking you for help. Just keeping you informed. But honestly, I don't know what to do next."

I am at a loss to suggest anything.

Dad interrupts my thoughts. "Your mother is coming downstairs. I have to go." The phone goes dead.

Poor Dad. I reflect that only a day ago I was identifying with Mom and assuming Dad was the cause of their problems. I remind myself that there's always another angle, an alternative story, where couples are concerned. Time to get on with my own life.

*

I phone Felicia to tell her where we haven't got to so far with Miguel.

"Let's ask Mr. Todd if he and Mr. Dan intervene for us with la migra?" she suggests.

Highly unlikely, I tell myself. But what use have I been so far?

"Is he in this morning?"

"Sí. Sí. I ask if he see us in one hour. Is that good?"

"I guess so. I'll be there by 10:30."

"Thank you. Thank you, preciosa."

Back in my Corolla I turn on KCRW. A commentator is talking about Dan Granger's stance on immigrants. Before the Gomez scandal he was slightly ahead of Jerry Brown in the polls. Now Brown has an overall ten-point lead over Granger.

I change channels. It's Kesha halfway through "TiK ToK"—

Tick-tock on the clock . . .

She's infectious. I want to be dancing as soon as I hear this party track. She's set on having a good time and offers no excuses for simply wanting to enjoy herself, turning and twisting to the music. I need to release the Kesha in myself. I need to do a lot of things. But first I have to make one last attempt to help Felicia.

"Hola!" a serious-faced Felicia greets me as I walk into the kitchen. "You arrive in time. Mr. Todd is waiting for us in the den."

She's changed. How? She seems more tentative than usual. More lost.

Todd is on the phone. He waves us in and points to two chairs facing his desk. "Can you confirm that a hundred thousand was deposited in my Number Two Business Checking Account this morning? Thank you. That's all for now. Goodbye."

Dirty money, I think.

"So what can I do for you?" Todd asks, looking from me to Felicia and back to me again.

"My nephew," Felicia blurts out. "La migra took him. ICE."

"I'm very sorry to hear that, Felicia. What was he arrested for?"

"We cannot find him," she replies without answering his question.

"Yes, but why was he arrested?" Todd asks again.

"He was charged with being in the US illegally," I interject.

"But he's been here all his life, hasn't he?"

"Sí. Sí." Felicia cries eagerly.

"What's his legal status?" Todd asks.

"I'm not sure," Felicia answers. "His mother says his number is not good."

"That's serious," Todd says. "But he still has the right to be heard by an immigration judge."

I shake my head. "Miguel signed away his rights to a hearing. He's facing fast-track deportation. We can't even find out which detention facility is holding him—"

Felicia breaks in. "Please, Mr. Todd. Your brother is important person in California. He can stop this."

Todd's demeanor changes.

"Felicia, I don't think you understand what you are asking."

"What you mean?"

"My brother is running for governor on a platform that promises to deport undocumented aliens. I can't possibly ask him to argue in favor of one."

"But Miguel is American," Felicia pleads. "He speak only English. He go to school here. He pay taxes."

"He's still illegal," Todd replies. "My brother can't help him without damaging his campaign."

"Please Mr. Todd. Help me. You are the only one that can help."

"I'm sorry, Felicia, but there's nothing I or my brother can do for your nephew. He should have applied for legal status a long time ago."

"But his parents don't have documents either."

"Then they should have done the same."

"Is not fair," Felicia says tearfully.

"I'm afraid life isn't always fair."

Felicia is sobbing now. She tries to speak, waves her hands, and rushes out of the room.

An instant later we hear a crash. Todd and I rush into the kitchen, where we find Felicia, still in tears, in the act of cleaning up a burnt soufflé she must have dropped as she was taking it out of the oven.

"I'm no better than Miguel," she says between sobs.

"What are you talking about, Felicia?" Todd asks.

"I'm illegal too. Like Miguel." she says.

"You've got a social security card," Todd says. "I've seen it."

"Miguel has one too," Felicia says. "Means nothing. I paid a Mexican lawyer for the card. Miguel too."

"You mean . . ." Todd shakes his head, as if to orient himself. "You're undocumented too?"

"Sí. Sí. And if Mr. Dan get elected I will be sent back too."

My heart sinks. Todd and I are shocked into a brief silence while we process this news. Felicia could become another Gomez.

Todd abruptly leaves the kitchen, and I follow him to the den. He dials a number on his cell phone—Dan's, I realize, as I listen to Todd explaining what he just heard to his brother.

"I know. That's why I phoned you . . . I agree . . . Of course . . . She's been with me for years now . . . Naturally you come first . . . Okay, I'll do it now . . . Don't worry. I'll make sure the press hears nothing about her . . . Leave it to me . . . Talk to you later . . . Bye."

"What are you going to do?" I ask, knowing the answer.

"What else can I do? I have to let her go."

"I can't believe you'd do that after all this time."

"Truly, I wish I didn't have to."

I follow him to the kitchen, where we find Felicia still crying.

"Felicia," Todd says, "I'm really sorry, but I cannot afford to let you continue working here. It will jeopardize my brother's career."

"What are you saying, Mr. Todd?" Felicia asks in a frightened voice.

"I mean that you are going to have to find a position somewhere else."

"You firing me?"

"I have to. I am giving you immediate notice. You've left me no choice."

Felicia breaks out in a new fit of sobbing.

"Can't you just ask her to take a break until after the election?" I ask.

"No. I can't. Even if he loses, my brother is a leading Republican politician with a strong stand on immigration. He can't be tainted by a brother employing an illegal immigrant. Felicia has to go. Now."

He turns back to Felicia. "I'm going to write you a check for three months' pay. On top of that I'm giving you a lump sum of $5,000. I hope that will give you time to find another job."

"I so sorry, Mr. Todd," Felicia sobs.

"I have just one condition, Felicia. An important one. You must never tell anyone that you worked for me. Is that understood?"

"Yes, Mr. Todd. I tell no one."

"Not even a friend."

"No, Mr. Todd."

"Good. I'll write you a check while you collect your things." Todd leaves the room.

"Poor Mr. Todd," Felicia says.

Poor Felicia, I think.

Todd has been generous enough, I reflect, unlike his brother's treatment of Gomez. And yet there was something too coldly efficient about his response. All his years with Felicia were erased in an instant. In his mind the money made it okay. How does he think she's going to get another job when she can't use him as a reference? She'll be forced to take on an after-hours cleaning job at some soulless office building—if she's lucky enough to find one. This is a side of Todd that I always assumed he must have. I'd just never seen it before. Yet I'm still shocked.

*

After I have helped a tearful Felicia gather her things together, load them in her trunk, and drive off, I go back into Todd's house and start watering the plants on the upper two floors. My eyes are filled with tears, whether from anger or sorrow I cannot determine.

On my way to the kitchen I bump into Todd coming out of the den. He avoids my eyes. He seems furtive somehow.

I hear the front door slam shut and Todd's car starting. I go to the den and make straight for the digital clock sitting on his desk. I rewind the hidden recording device five minutes' worth and press PLAY. Todd is talking to Jorge, telling him what has just transpired between him and Felicia.

"You can see how potentially damaging this news could be to Dan's campaign. Who knows how Felicia will feel once she's absorbed what's happened to her."

"Women change with the wind," Jorge says.

"Dan says he can't risk trusting Felicia not to tell someone that she worked for me as an illegal. If that leaks, all hell will break loose."

"Yes?" Jorge prods him.

"I need you to smuggle her out of the country—today."

"I see," Jorge stalls.

"I will pay you generously for your trouble."

"Define 'generously.'"

"Would ten grand do it?"

"How about twenty?" Jorge is no pushover.

"Let's not quibble. Split the difference. Fifteen."

"Sounds good. So where do I find her?"

Todd gives Jorge her address in East LA.

"So, you'll do it this afternoon?"

"Don't you worry. Better you know as little about the logistics as possible."

"Yes. You're right—"

I hear the front door slam. Damn it! Todd's back already. What to do? With no time to think I snatch the SD card from the device, close it, and slip silently out of the den as he is still moving around the entrance hall. I leave by the kitchen door.

As soon as I start my car, I regret my hasty action. Unless I can get the card back into the recording device, it will be missed. Especially if it is being accessed remotely via Wi-Fi.

More importantly, I have to warn Felicia that she's going to be kidnapped at any minute. I call her cell.

"Hola!"

"Felicia. It's me, Jenny."

"Sí, Jenny. Que pasa?"

She doesn't sound like her normal self.

"How are you feeling?" I ask.

"Horrible, por supuesto."

She bursts out crying.

"Where are you now?"

"Home," she manages between sobs.

"You have to leave. *Now*."

"What?"

"Todd asked Jorge to have you kidnapped and taken to Mexico. He asked Jorge to do it now."

"Now?" Felicia sounds panicky.

"He could be on his way to your house as I speak."

"Where do I go?"

"I'll call Eduardo right after this call and ask him to hide you while we sort this out."

"But I need time for my things."

"There's no time for that, Felicia. This is serious. You have to get out of your house *now*. Just grab whatever you can."

"Sí. Rápidamente." But Felicia doesn't sound in a hurry. She's too confused.

"You've got ten minutes," I say, pulling the figure out of the air.

"Ten minutes."

"Then drive away and keep driving until I call you."

"Okay, okay. Gracias, Jenny. You are very good."

"And don't answer the phone to anyone except me. They can trace you that way. Okay?"

"Sí, sí. No worry. I won't."

"In fact, shut your phone down completely."

"I do it now."

"I promise I'll be in touch with you very soon. Now get yourself out of there."

I end the call and find myself shaking violently. Poor Felicia. If only she hadn't confessed to Todd. If only—

Time to stop these useless regrets.

*

Still sitting in my car parked in Todd's driveway I call Eduardo and tell him what's going on.

"Poor Felicia," he says.

"Can you help me find somewhere that I can send Felicia to? Somewhere where she'll be safe for the moment?"

"That I certainly can do. We frequently have to help immigrants disappear before starting their life again."

"Where do you have in mind?"

"A room in an apartment in Boyle Heights."

"Thank you, Eduardo. You are a jewel . . . Who lives in this apartment?" I ask after a pause.

"My great-aunt, as a matter of fact. Her name's Gloria. She's lived there since the seventies. I pay half her rent, and in return she takes in any of my clients as needed."

"Felicia should be in less danger after the polls close tomorrow."

"No hurry. We'll take it day by day."

"It's just that I know she won't want to impose longer than she has to. She's fiercely independent."

"I'll phone Aunt Gloria and let her know Felicia is coming." He gives me Gloria's address and phone number.

"What are you up to now?" he asks.

"I have to put in some hours today at Total Surveillance."

"Maybe we can do something together this evening?" Eduardo suggests.

My heart races. "That would be nice," I say.

"I'll call you later. Hasta luego," and he hangs up.

I call Felicia back and give her Eduardo's aunt's address. Reaching the obvious conclusion that I cannot return the SD card anytime soon to its place in Todd's den, I start my car and set out for Century City.

*

Back at my viewing station at Total Surveillance I'm tracking a young woman from the Westside suspected of having an affair, when Grant calls and asks me to come up to his office at once. He doesn't sound his usual urbane self.

I enter his capacious office. He is sitting in his upholstered executive office chair behind an enormous leather-topped desk with only a laptop, cell phone, and desk lamp on it. He doesn't ask me to sit down.

"What can I do for you?" I ask with a catch in my throat.

"Roberto, who regularly replaces SD cards for us, just phoned me to say that the video from Todd's den has gone missing. As you know about the devices in his house I wondered whether you could throw any light on this development."

I curse myself for panicking and not taking the time to replace the recording in the clock and wind it to its latest endpoint. I quickly come up with a lie.

"As a matter of fact, I can," I say. "Felicia, the housekeeper who discovered the cam in the kitchen, confronted Todd and asked him why he was spying on her. When Todd asked her what she was talking about she showed him the device concealed in the photo frame. He was stunned. And concerned. He went on a hunt throughout the house, and when I left this morning he was watching all the videos. He might have taken the recording from the clock in his den to watch at his office when Roberto slipped in to replace it. At least that's my best guess."

"This is not good news," Grant says. "Broken confidentiality. Possible end of contract. A real shit-storm in the making."

"I could be wrong. I'm just guessing what might have caused its disappearance."

"I know. I know," Grant says irritably. "But you're the only one who knew where the devices were."

Is this an accusation? I choose to take it as a statement of fact.

"And Felicia. And now also Todd."

Grant's cell phone rings, and he answers it.

After a moment he puts his phone on speaker while placing his finger over his lips to caution me to stay silent. Todd's voice fills the room.

"I need you to find out the whereabouts of my housekeeper Felicia. Turns out she has no working papers. She's an illegal immigrant. I was forced to let her go this morning. As you know, my brother is running for the governor's office. We can't afford a scandal because a family member employed undocumented aliens."

Aliens! That is how he refers to Felicia, a trusted employee of all those years. Interesting, too, that Todd doesn't trust Jorge to find Felicia, instead attempting to double up his chance of success.

"I've tried calling her three times in the past hour, but I'm getting no answer," Todd adds.

"I see," Grant says. "So . . . what's her home address? We can start there."

Todd gives him Felicia's address, cell phone number, and email address.

"One more thing," Grant says. "If she was afraid that you were taping her, she might not pick up on your calls."

"Taping her?" Todd repeats. "What do you mean?"

Uh-oh! I think.

"Jenny told me that Felicia had accused you today of secretly recording her conversations" Grant says. "That might have made her think you were planning to have her deported."

"Felicia did no such thing," Todd says hotly. "I'm confused. What recordings are you talking about?"

Grant looks daggers at me.

"The fact is that Total Surveillance was engaged by a client who was concerned with Susan's disappearance," he tells Todd. "We installed concealed cameras in your house to see if any light might be shed on her whereabouts."

"This is quite outrageous," Todd says. "Who's the client?"

"You know that's confidential," Grant says. "But I can assure you the investigation had nothing to do with you. Our client was solely focused on finding out where Susan might be hiding out."

Todd says, "You realize that I could sue you, Grant?"

After a moment, Grant says, "To make it up to you I'll take on the search for Felicia at no charge. What do you say?"

"That is the least you can do. And make sure you have those devices removed from my home today."

"Of course I will," Grant says. "I really do apologize."

There's silence on the line. Then Todd says, "What was Jenny talking about, anyway? Felicia never mentioned any recording to me."

Looking at me, Grant says, "I have no idea. You'll have to ask Jenny that. She'll be here working for another hour."

In an icy voice, Todd says, "Tell Jenny to come to my house when she's done working. I need to talk to her this evening."

"I'll make sure she gets the message," Grant says, glaring at me. "Meantime, I'll immediately put someone on the trail of Felicia."

"And remember to send someone else to recover the recordings."

"I sure will. As soon as I have any news I'll be in touch with you."

"Make sure you do that," Todd responds curtly and hangs up.

Grant turns to me, his face contorted with rage.

"What the hell is going on? Why are you lying to me?"

I'm feeling doubly guilty now, for lying and for landing Grant in trouble with an important client.

"I'm truly sorry, Grant. You see I've been trying to locate the whereabouts of Susan for days. And it was Felicia who told me about the recording devices in Todd's house—"

"You're not explaining why you lied to me," Grant interrupts me.

I can't let him know that I'd seen the recording of the meeting between Todd and Jorge. Jorge is his client, and Grant would more than likely tell him that I had overheard that conversation, which would make me a target of the cartel. It could well put me in physical danger. Even threaten my life.

"I'm sorry. I can't," I mumble, looking down at my lap.

"You can't! Why on earth not?"

"Because it would break my client's confidentiality."

"So you've now got your own client?"

"I promise you, this is the last thing I wanted to happen."

"But it has happened."

I stay silent, as I cannot deny this.

"Hasn't it?"

"Yes, it has. I'm really sorry, Grant."

"Sorry doesn't do it, I'm afraid."

He phones a number and asks whoever it is to come up to his office. We sit in awkward silence until the door opens and Alexandro, the duty security officer, appears.

"Alexandro, please accompany Ms. Carter to her position in the viewing room and see that she leaves with only her personal belongings. She is not to be allowed back in the building after that."

"You're firing me?" I stammer.

"You've left me no choice. You will receive your termination check in the mail. Now leave."

As I walk through the door that Alexandro is holding open for me, Grant is dialing a number. I have already become an annoying memory to him, just as Felicia was wiped clean from Todd's consciousness this morning. Everyone is expendable, I remind myself. And not just as an employee (part-time at that). I'm physically expendable too.

Suddenly I feel terrified. Powerful forces are swirling around me, and they could sweep me up, as the wind does a fallen leaf. Who was Grant phoning? Jorge? That would be really bad news for me.

Alexandro doesn't say a word. I'm sure he's been through this process many times. I pick up the few personal items I've got in my kiosk, put them in my shoulder bag, and go to the garage. Under Alexandro's sad watchful gaze, I leave Total Surveillance, another redundant employee to be dismissed and forgotten.

*

When I'm a few blocks from Total Surveillance I pull my car over to the curb. I'm shaken, and I need to think. Now, how am I going to pay my rent? But that's not my primary concern. What worries me most is that I feel directly under threat.

Thanks to the recording I took from Todd's den, there's no doubt about Dan and his brother's connection to the drug cartel. If that became public it would threaten Todd, Dan, and Jorge. Jorge! He's a leading member of a gang that regularly murders people to protect its turf and its profits.

I'm in big trouble. I'm trembling, and sweat is running down my face.

The card is the key. If I surrender it to them I'll lose the only leverage I have. I need to leave the card somewhere safe. Of course! Eduardo.

I call him at work and tell him what's happened.

"You're not thinking of doing what Todd has asked and going back to his place, are you?" he asks.

"Yes. But only after I've left the cards with you to guarantee my safe return."

"How do you mean?" He sounds guarded.

"If you don't hear from me by eight this evening I want you to take the cards to the *Los Angeles Times*."

"Why are you putting yourself in danger?" He sounds genuinely worried.

"Because if I don't meet up with them, I will be seen as a danger to the cartel. I can't hide from the cartel for the rest of my life. I have to negotiate an exchange that will remove me from their sights for good."

"What if Jorge and his men try forcing you to hand over the recording?"

"That's why I want you to leave for the *Times* at eight promptly." I'm terrified, but I try to keep my fear out of my voice.

"You've really thought this thing through."

"Only as I'm talking to you."

"I'm impressed."

There is a brief silence. I continue:

"I want to leave the card with you, plus the copies I made of the earlier ones from Todd's rooms downstairs. I need to recover them from home first."

"By then I'll be at Aunt Gloria's place."

"Okay. I'll get there as soon as I can."

"See you then. Be careful."

"I'm trying to be. Thank you."

*

As I let myself into the apartment I momentarily lose my new feeling of acute anxiety as I hear Tricia's voice on the phone to someone. It must be a client; she's using her professional voice—wanting to please without sounding obsequious. I wish she'd sometimes use it with me. I'm not holding my breath.

"—That sounds perfect," Tricia is saying. "Apart from other considerations it saves you fifty thousand dollars. I truly believe this is the best offer we will get." I admiringly note her use of "we." "I'll see you then in my office tomorrow at 10. We'll have the papers ready for you to sign. I'm very happy for you. . . Goodbye."

Happy for herself, I think. But why should I begrudge her a sale? The last thing I want to become is bitchy like her. I get into my room, take out the SD card and copy it on my duplicator. I should have left it in place, dammit.

"So what's going on?" Tricia asks from my bedroom doorway.

"I just got fired by Total Surveillance," I say nonchalantly, as I remove the card from the SD card duplicator.

"I don't know whether to commiserate with you or congratulate you."

"Neither do I," I say, while searching for the earlier copies I made of the cards from Todd's house.

"What are you doing?"

"I need to take some surveillance recordings to Eduardo."

"Oh! Eduardo! He's becoming a hot item in your schedule, isn't he?"

"So?"

"You need to slow down a bit."

"Why?"

"Because Eduardo can't be that well off."

"Is that all that you can think of?" I reply angrily.

"Actually, no."

"What, then?"

"Why are you getting yourself mixed up with someone who's obsessed with helping illegal immigrants?"

"They're not necessarily illegal. Just undocumented."

"Oh, we're clutching at straws now, are we?"

"What's wrong with doing what Eduardo does?"

"Nothing if you're Mexican."

"He's not Mexican. He's American."

"You know what I mean."

"No, I don't."

"Alright," Tricia sits on my bed. "What I would like to know is, why you're getting yourself involved in the problems of Mexicans. Don't you have enough problems as it is?"

"So it's Mexicans that bother you?"

"You've just unshackled yourself from one of the bums of this world, and now you want to attach yourself to another problem? Can't you give yourself a break?"

"What makes you think Eduardo's a problem? He's CEO of the Coalition for Immigrants' Rights."

"He's totally focused on his people, who have no right to be in our country in the first place."

"No right?

"They've broken our laws. They identify with their own country. They send all their cash back to where they came from. They only want our money."

"You sound like Dan Granger."

"He's one of the few politicians in this state who makes any sense. He calls them illegal because that's what they are."

"He's a creep and a hypocrite. Besides, Eduardo isn't illegal."

"But he defends people who break the law."

"He defends people who are so desperate to feed their families that they risk everything to come here and try to provide for them."

"They should be staying in their own country and forcing their own government to pay them a living wage."

"For god's sake," I snap at Tricia, "we're all the descendants of immigrants."

"Just don't think of bringing your lover of criminals to my apartment. He's not welcome here."

"You can't tell me who I can bring home to my own place."

Tricia rises from the bed, eyes blazing.

"It's not your place. It's mine. I've tried to help you out by letting you stay here for a small rental—"

"SMALL!"

"You think you could find your own place for what you pay me?"

"To hell with you. No one is going to tell me who I can bring home."

"Fine! Good luck finding your own place. You're going to have to work 18 hours a day just to cover the rent."

"That's it. I'm leaving tonight. I'll get the rest of my things when I've sorted myself out."

"That's exactly what you need to do. Sort yourself out."

"Fuck off."

"My pleasure." Tricia goes into her bedroom and slams the door.

I'm really mad at her. My own sister a bigot! I've tried to hide this part of her from my conscious self. Now that's no longer possible. I can't continue sharing an apartment with her. I have no choice, especially when the object of her bigotry is Eduardo. Hell!

I start throwing clothes into my suitcase. Lulu rubs herself against me, purring, as if she knows I'm leaving and not coming back. I grab my stuff from the bathroom, and pack up my aging laptop and the cards from Todd's house. After sitting on my suitcase to close it, I storm out of the apartment and slam the front door behind me.

Now what?

*

I sit in my old car outside the apartment without turning on the engine. Much as I hate to admit it, Tricia's right. I need to sort my life out. And today may be the day I am forced to do just that. First, I get fired. Then I make myself homeless. And now I am about to confront

Todd and probably lose my other part-time job. That's quite impressive for a day's work.

And yet I feel inexplicably exhilarated. I knew I had to upend my life if I wasn't going to waste it getting by on near-minimum wages, projecting my feelings onto Gary, and living at my sister's, subject to her whims and needs.

I'm filled with conflicting emotions—fear of what awaits me at Todd's, and excitement facing an unknown future; fear about how I'm going to pay my way, and relief at ending my dependence on low-paid part-time jobs; fear of becoming homeless, but grateful to be free of Tricia's constant criticism. I've burnt my bridges now; I can only move forward to a future still obscured by the mess I've gotten myself into.

Why does change feel so painful? I now see that continuing my previous way of life had become impossible well before today. It just took today for my actions to catch up with my inner convictions. It's as if my unconscious has finally taken charge of my everyday self. Enough! it tells me. You can be so much better than who you are. You can do so much better than what you've been doing. Yet I'm shaking. On the point of tears. Terrified.

Nonetheless, it's time to move forward. I turn on the ignition and start driving toward Boyle Heights. On NPR, wouldn't you know it, they're talking about immigration. "In Los Angeles County, one-third of the residents are immigrants, nearly half the workforce is foreign-born, two-thirds of children have at least one immigrant parent, and 90 percent of those youngsters are US-born. How these children and their parents fare will determine the future of the region."

A Pulitzer Prize–winning columnist points out that according to a recent CNN poll, 25% of the American people still don't believe that President Obama was born in the United States. We live in an age in which strong opinions overwhelm facts, he says.

Dan asserts that a substantial number of immigrants have committed crimes, and the media treats this lie with as much space and time as the truth, which is that a lower percentage of illegal immigrants commit crimes than do native-born US citizens.

*

Eduardo's aunt Gloria lives in the upstairs apartment of a duplex. I park in front of a local laundromat in hopes of deterring locals from trashing my old Corolla. As I haul my suitcase out of the trunk a teenage boy in white T-shirt, black baggy pants with split cuffs, and a red bandana tied round his forehead asks me, "Movin' in?" I shake my head as I walk past him to Gloria's entrance. "I'd give you twenty bucks for half an hour," he calls after me.

I ring the doorbell. A cracked woman's voice issuing from the rusting speaker vent asks, "Who's there?" I give my name, the buzzer sounds, and I push open the front door. I grope my way up a concrete staircase dimly lit by a bare bulb regulated by a loudly ticking timer. Halfway up the light clicks off.

When I reach the upper landing, Eduardo opens the door.

He gives me a restrained hug. "Why are you dragging around a suitcase? Planning a trip?"

"Sounds like a good idea," I reply. "Let me in and I'll tell you the whole sad story."

I step into a world of vibrant colors—magenta walls, lemon yellow ceiling, painted wooden furniture, lots of Zapotec rugs. Haphazardly colored wool animals tumble over each other on one shelf. On the shelf above there's a Day of the Dead tableau. On the wall hangs a picture of a folk Virgin gesturing towards her immaculate heart in a massive gold frame. The living room is furnished with a variety of chairs, a carved dark-brown coffee table, and an old Spanish-style wooden cabinet.

"Meet my favorite aunt," says Eduardo.

"Mucho gusto," I greet her.

"Delighted to meet you too," she replies in perfect English.

We grin at one another over her gentle correction of my assumption that she speaks only Spanish.

Gloria must be in her late sixties. She still has a sparkle in her brown eyes, wears her black hair tied in a loose bun, and walks with a slight limp, as she comes forward to greet me warmly with a long hug.

Felicia waves at me from a dilapidated armchair draped in a Oaxacan blanket, in which she is sitting at the far end of the room while sipping at a bottle of berry juice. I go over to her, bend over, grasp her by the shoulders, and kiss her on each cheek. She clasps me round the shoulders.

"¡Dios mio!" she exclaims. "What to do."

"Nothing for the time being," I tell her. "It is not over."

"Sí. Sí," is all she says with a big sigh.

Eduardo's cell phone rings. A woman's voice is shouting something. He moves into an inner room as he answers.

"Didn't I ask you not to call me? Why is it . . ."

I can't hear the rest. Gloria looks concerned, so she must know whom he's talking to. Eduardo soon returns to the room and mutters an apology. I get the feeling he's apologizing for not being open about the call. Is he involved with a woman? I ask myself. Am I just imagining a special connection between us?

I tell Eduardo about my fight with Tricia. He sympathizes, saying that he has a brother in Texas with whom he has a similar adversarial relationship. I ask him what his brother does.

"He's an insurance executive, very straight and boring."

"Has he got family?" I ask.

"A wife and daughter, and another child on the way. Plus a three-bedroom house and a Lincoln SUV. Complete assimilation is what he wants—even if he'll never achieve it."

"Tricia has only one goal in life—to make money. Lots of it. Preferably by attracting rich men."

"Sounds as if she has already achieved her goal," Eduardo says.

"Then what's she going to do for the remainder of her life?"

"The same, but with diminishing success," he replies.

Eduardo and I are so on the same wavelength, I reflect. And, without meaning to, he's helped me understand why I resist Tricia's belief in always putting herself first. Reciprocity counts. I am as much a social being as an individual.

But I hardly know Eduardo. I could be all wrong about this. What was that phone call about, for example?

Gloria offers me a cold drink, and I accept.

I hand Eduardo all the recording cards I copied, including today's.

I say to him, "If you don't hear from me by 8 this evening I want you to deliver these to the *LA Times* and fill in a reporter with the background story."

"Now you've got me really worried," he says.

"These cards are my insurance. They guarantee my safety."

"Not if you find yourself dealing with the cartel, I can assure you."

"Trust me. Todd is not into physical violence."

"I'm more worried about Jorge. He may be the cartel's financial CEO, but he's Pablo Valdez's brother, and Pablo is a known killer."

"Come on. I'm going to see Todd, not Pablo Valdez."

"They're all connected. I don't want anything to happen to you when I'm only just getting to know you."

Is he saying what I hope he's saying? "I appreciate that."

"I can see you're set on driving down to Newport Beach. Let me go with you."

I am sorely tempted. But I know that I have got to face them alone to convince them that I am no threat to them once we've agreed on terms. This is something only I can do to safeguard my own future.

"Thank you. But I have to do this on my own."

"Okay. I wish it wasn't so. At least let me carry your case down to the car."

"Thank you."

"Where are you going to sleep tonight?" Eduardo asks as he's loading my suitcase in the trunk.

"I haven't thought that far ahead."

"Why not come to my place?" Eduardo says. "I have a spare bedroom with its own bathroom."

I can hardly believe it. I never expected this to happen so soon in my wildest dreams.

But I reply, "That's a generous offer, but I'm sure I can go to my parents' for the night." What's with me?

"You would be doing me a favor. I want the chance to spend time with you. We need time to talk over dinner. Please. I'm being utterly selfish. I'm asking you to do this for my sake."

Thankfully I relent. "Well, thank you, Eduardo. I too look forward to talking together." Talking! I exclaim to myself. I want to pull him hard against me and feel the length of his body pressed against mine.

He asks me for my phone and enters his address in my map app.

We hug each other briefly. Then I get in my car and drive off. In the rear mirror I see him gazing after me until I turn the corner.

What is it he is so anxious to talk about? Is it about the woman on the other end of the line?

En route to Newport Beach, I turn on the radio and am plunged into the election debate. "Addressing a crowd of supporters in San Diego's Old Town this morning, Governor Brown charged candidate Dan Granger with a lack of experience. 'If we claim we're going to run California like a business, shouldn't we review the resumes of those who want to be the governor?' he said to cheers and laughs from the audience. 'If we look at the resume and there's nothing on it, it's totally blank, shouldn't we tell the candidate, you need to seek other work, because you have no qualifications for this position?'"

"Meanwhile Dan Granger was addressing a crowd of Republican election workers in Costa Mesa: 'Thank you, everyone, for all you have done for me and for California. Don't listen to the pollsters. The only numbers that count are the votes tomorrow. There are going to be a lot of surprised folks by the end of the day after all the votes have been tallied. We'll make this state great again.' He was greeted with chants of 'Mr. Governor!'"

"Slime ball!" I yell at the car radio and turn it off.

I need to plan for my confrontation with Todd. Do I even want to keep my part-time job with him? A spirit of recklessness possesses me. I feel I need to make a complete break with my old life. But I still have no idea what I will say to Todd when I get there. At least I have a contingency plan should I run into real danger because of what I know. Tonight I might get to see what he's really like beneath that smooth, charming veneer. The two brothers seem so different in personality. But are their actions so different?

For relief I tune in to KCSN's Afternoon Music Mix. They're playing Crosby and Nash's "Immigration Man": "I got stopped by the Immigration Man / He says he doesn't know if he can / Let me in— let me in—immigration man." That song must date from the 1970s. How long will it go on being relevant? So many Miguels. So many Felicias. How long?

*

I am at Todd's front door. I press the bell. It's 6:40. Suddenly the door swings open and Todd stands in the doorway.

"Come in," he says peremptorily. He turns his back on me, and I follow him into the kitchen. Now I am nothing more than an errant worker in his eyes.

He perches on a tall stool and leaves me standing. "So what is this story about Felicia accusing me of secretly recording her conversations? I only learned from Grant today that someone had paid him to put recording devices in my house."

"I only learned about the recordings myself on Saturday." Could it be that recently? "Felicia found a video recording device in the kitchen. She asked me about it because she didn't know what it was."

"Go on."

"When I looked at it I recognized the logo on the SD card. It was from Total Surveillance. So the next time I was at work I looked up the card, and it turned out to be one of a series of devices planted throughout your house."

"Why didn't you tell me immediately?"

"I was faced with a conflict of interest, as I worked for both you and Grant."

"And you chose to protect Grant at my expense?"

"I didn't see it that way."

"And how did you see it?"

"Circumstances have changed now. I'm no longer an employee of Total Surveillance. Grant fired me this afternoon because I lied to him. That was because I had removed a card from your den and couldn't replace it in time. Grant's operative informed him that the card had gone missing and that someone must know about their surveillance. As Grant knew I worked for you, he asked me if I could explain the card's disappearance, and I made up that stupid lie that was quickly exposed as one."

"Well, now that you don't work for him you can tell me who commissioned the surveillance in the first place."

Should I tell him? Why not? I owe Grant nothing. And it might set him at odds with Jorge and the cartel.

"It was Jorge Valdez."

"Jorge Valdez! Are you certain?"

"That was the name on the Security Agreement at Total Surveillance."

"Why would Jorge bug my house?"

"I don't know."

After a prolonged silence Todd asks, "So how much do you know from watching the recording?"

I hesitate. Do I lie again? That didn't do me much good last time.

"I know that you asked Jorge to kidnap Felicia and take her across the border." Silence.

I summon my courage. "How could you do that?"

"Have you any idea what the press would do if they knew I had employed an illegal immigrant all this time?"

"You should know that Felicia would never tell anyone."

"It would finish my brother's bid for the governor's job," Todd continues, ignoring my objection.

"And what do you think having her kidnapped by a Mexican cartel would do to his campaign?" I burst out. Mistake. I've let him know that I know Jorge's connection to a cartel.

Todd shakes his head. "You are so naive, Jenny."

To my surprise I remain defiant. "At least I'm not kidnapping people and collaborating with foreign gangs."

"It's for Felicia's good as well as the campaign's."

"I don't follow."

"She'd get a significant settlement sum to compensate her for the inconvenience."

"But she would be terrified of what might happen to her," I protest.

"In return for a short stay in Mexico, she would receive what would be for her a large chunk of money," Todd replies.

"How long would that last when she couldn't find another well-paid job?" I ask.

"This is all beside the point," Todd says with exasperation, "since we can't find her." He thrusts his face an inch from mine. "Do you know where she is?"

"If I did know," I lie, "I wouldn't tell you."

Todd's face darkens. "You're playing with fire, Jenny. This is far too serious to be playing games like this."

"What you are asking Jorge to do is not just illegal. It's unethical."

"The modern world doesn't work like that. What matters today is money—and power, because money creates power. Money enables those who have it to help those less fortunate—"

"—Like Felicia?" I ask sarcastically.

"Yes, dammit! Like Felicia."

"So you trust Jorge, someone who has secretly been recording everything going on in your home, but won't trust Felicia, who has been loyal to you for all these years?"

"You'll learn one day that you never trust anyone in this life," Todd says. "Everyone has a price. Everyone can be bought."

"I never took you to be such a cynic."

"I'm a realist."

Todd stands up. "Let's go ask Jorge why he bugged my house."

Todd shepherds me across the hall and into the den. The light from a desk lamp casts elongated shadows on the walls and the carpeted floor. I dimly discern Jorge and Dan, sitting beside one another in matching armchairs, sipping Scotch from crystal tumblers.

Dan looks up at me. "The flower girl!" he says in his smarmy voice.

Ignoring his brother, Todd says to Jorge, "Meet Jenny, who does my plant maintenance."

"Muy hermosa!" Jorge remarks, as if I wasn't in the room. I stare back at the two of them.

Todd helps himself to a generous shot of whiskey. He doesn't offer me any.

"Jenny works part-time at Total Surveillance," Todd tells Jorge. "She tells me that you had them place recording devices all over my house. Is that true?"

"What?" says Dan.

"There's no point in my denying it," Jorge shrugs, without offering any apology.

"And exactly what were you hoping to discover?" Todd asks acidly.

"Whether Felicia knew about the connection between the cartel and the two of you," Jorge replies. "I had all our interests in mind."

"Then why didn't you tell me you were doing it?" Todd asks.

"Because the CEO of Total Surveillance advised me that the fewer individuals who knew about it the likelier it would remain a secret."

"Really?" Todd remarks cynically.

"Look at how soon it has become an open secret," Jorge points out.

"And does Felicia know about the connection between you and me?" Todd asks Jorge.

"We found no evidence that she does."

"That's just as well," Todd says, "as your guys seem unable to locate her whereabouts."

"It's only a matter of time before we find her," Jorge responds. "We're hot on her trail." I hope you're bragging, I tell him silently.

"Hot or cold, it is little more than thirteen hours before the polling stations open," Dan says.

No one says anything for a minute.

Jorge turns to me, "How many cards have you seen?"

"A number," I say evasively.

"Which ones?"

"From the kitchen, the den, and the living room."

"And why have you been watching them?"

"Because Felicia asked me to find out what has happened to Susan."

"Now she thinks she's a detective," Dan sneers.

"Felicia wouldn't take no for an answer," I tell Todd. "You know how attached she'd become to Susan." Todd remains detached and noncommittal.

"So," Jorge continues, "what did the recordings tell you about Susan?"

"Nothing that helped. Apart from today's recording, I only saw recordings from Saturday."

"So," Todd jumps on my admission, "you heard the conversation I had with Jorge about our financial arrangements?" Todd asks.

"Yes," I say, flushing with inner anger.

I turn on Dan. "You're such a hypocrite. Publicly you're targeting illegal immigrants. Secretly you're financing your campaign with the support of a cartel that makes millions of dollars smuggling immigrants into the country?"

"The end result is the only thing that counts," Dan says. "Where we get the money from is secondary."

"You're disgusting," I say.

"Happily, I don't have to worry about liberal extremists like you," he replies.

"Yes you do. You need our votes."

"There are plenty of Californians who want illegal immigrants sent back to where they came from."

Todd intervenes. "Enough about politics. Jenny, I want those recordings back."

"I only have the card from your den today," I lie. "Besides, why should I give it to you?"

"Because it belongs to me. Actually, legally speaking, it belongs to Jorge."

Jorge chimes in. "Yes," he says, "we want the SD card returned now."

"And what if I refuse?"

Todd addresses Dan. "Perhaps we should leave this matter to Jorge. It's his area of expertise, isn't it?"

Dan nods, and the two of them take their drinks out of the den. Jorge glares at me menacingly. Now I'm really scared.

*

"Sit," Jorge says, pointing at the chair facing the desk. When I hesitate he grabs my shoulders and shoves me into it. I'm shaking now out of fear and anger. But I'm not about to let Jorge know.

"What do you think you're doing?" I ask.

"Not much so far," he replies menacingly.

I look for a diversion. "Why did you really plant those recording devices?" I ask.

"Are you saying you don't believe what I told Todd?"

"How can I?" I say, smiling and recrossing my legs in a flirtatious manner. "You started recording long before you entered into a financial arrangement with Todd and Dan. August the third, to be exact."

"I'm impressed. You've done your homework." He pauses, considering this. "I see no harm in telling you."

Maybe flirtation works with him. Then, he adds:

"One way or another you won't be in any position to act as a witness."

My heart misses a beat. What does he mean? Still, he continues:

"Susan began pestering Todd about his and Dan's connection to me and the cartel. Todd held out for as long as he could. But in early August she overheard a telephone conversation between Todd and me about a major financial deal. When she confronted Todd he admitted that the cartel wanted to buy into his hedge fund, and that he was considering saying yes."

"And that was enough to drive Susan away?" I ask, looking directly into his eyes.

"Not on its own. When Susan pressed him about Dan's role in that, she found out that he would receive a large campaign contribution. That's when she blew up and moved out."

"So why should that concern you?" I ask.

Jorge hesitates, then decides to humor me. "Because Susan worked for Eduardo Muñez at the Coalition for Immigrants' Rights. If she told him what she knew we would all be in danger of exposure."

"And what was your solution?"

"Let us say that we removed Susan from any contact with Eduardo."

"Removed? What are you saying?"

"I've told you too much already." Jorge puts his drink down on the desk with a bang.

"Where is she?" I ask.

"I have no more to say on that subject."

"But . . . but why continue the recordings?"

"We had to find out whether Susan had told Felicia what she knew."

"And how do you think Todd would react if he knew you 'removed' Susan?"

"He's not going to know."

"What's to stop me telling him?" I instantly regret my words.

Jorge moves closer, towering above me. "I don't think you realize how precarious your present situation is," he growls. "I can't release you until you've given me all the evidence you have of the cartel's connection to Todd and Dan. Even then I will need to keep you until after the polls close tomorrow."

"You're threatening to lock me up for the next 24 hours?"

"That's the minimum option."

"And the maximum?"

"I leave that up to your imagination."

I've experienced fear before, but never have I been in fear for my life. "If I tell you where the card is that connects your money to the Grangers, will you let me leave?"

"First I would need to see and verify the card."

"And then?"

"We'll see. You're in no position to bargain, you know."

"Then there is no reason for me to give you the card."

Jorge bends over me menacingly. "I can make you hand over the card."

"And how do you propose doing that?" I sound a lot cooler than I feel inside.

"You wouldn't really want to lose your sight, would you? Or be disfigured for life with a scar running across your face?"

I can feel my hands gripping the arms of my chair as if my life depended on it. "And once you free me how do you expect to avoid the consequences of what you've done?"

"From the Federales? What a joke. They can be bought off for 2,000 pesos."

"The Federales? Mexico!" Hell!

"But all that is unnecessary," Jorge says coolly. "Just tell me where to find the card. Then we can discuss your future."

What are my options? I can afford to play the single card and see what he does in return. I fish the original card out of my jeans pocket and hand it to Jorge.

He reads the Total Surveillance ID on the back and inserts it into the recording device concealed in the digital clock on the desk. He keeps the sound on low so that I can't overhear it, alternating between fast forward and play. After a few minutes, he extracts the card and puts it into his wallet.

"Now are you satisfied?" I ask.

"Should I be?" he asks quizzically.

"You tell me," I reply guardedly.

Jorge makes a gesture with his hand as if swatting away a fly. "The question remains: did you make a copy of this?"

"No I didn't," I lie.

"How am I to know you're telling the truth?"

I shrug. "Beats me."

"Then I will have to detain you for the time being."

A wave of icy terror runs through me. "You never intended to release me."

"Not until the polls close," he says with a twisted grin.

*

Suddenly Todd bursts through the door with Roberto in tow.

"Total Surveillance sent Roberto over to remove all the recording devices from my home," Todd tells Jorge. Jorge nods noncommittally.

Using a screwdriver Roberto starts removing the mechanism from the clock. As he is placing the device in his carry bag and preparing to leave, I say: "Roberto, could you please give me a lift back with you?"

Before Roberto can respond, Jorge says. "Jenny and I still have business to conclude. Thank you, Roberto. That will be all."

"We can do our business in the morning," I say, trying to hide the desperation I'm feeling.

"We will do it now," Jorge says, staring aggressively at Roberto.

Roberto looks from Jorge to me, then leaves the room with Todd.

"Nice try," Jorge remarks sarcastically.

After a moment's reflection Jorge remarks, "What I don't fully understand is why you still seem so confident. Once you are in Mexico you will be in the hands of cartel members who are used to solving problems by violent means. What have you got up your sleeve?"

Time to play my trump card. "You haven't asked me whether I made copies of the cards I found at Total Surveillance on Saturday."

"I take it that means that you did," Jorge responds quickly.

"You are correct." I try to look confident.

"How many copies?"

"Five."

"Then we will need to recover those this evening. Where are the cards? Are you also carrying those around with you?"

"I'm not an idiot," I say. "You've already proved to me that you don't stand by your word once you have what you want."

"Where are they?" Jorge repeats impatiently.

"Somewhere safe," I say.

Jorge wraps his hands around my neck "Quit playing games," he snarls. "I want to know where the cards are. Now."

Half choking, I manage to reply, "I left them with someone who will deliver them to the *LA Times* if I don't show up in person by 8 tonight."

"Fuck!" Jorge shouts, letting go of my throat.

"I still have time to make it back safely by then."

"It's not that easy, idiota," he replies angrily. "Do you think I am going to let you go free without a guarantee that you'll give me the cards tonight?"

"And how do you plan to get that guarantee?" I ask.

"It wouldn't take long for one of my guys to extract the information from you. They're very practiced at that sort of thing."

My stomach churns.

"By then the *LA Times* will have got the cards. Also a condition is that I show up in person *unharmed* by 8."

Jorge steps back and leans against the desk. "So, we need to negotiate. I have already said that I need to be a hundred percent certain that those cards go nowhere except to me."

"I understand that," I say. "I will give them to you first thing tomorrow morning. Clearly I have no interest in endangering my life by giving the cards to anyone else. For my part, you three keep telling me that money matters. I don't want any money for myself. What I want is, firstly, a guarantee that you will leave me and Felicia alone once this deal is over—"

"—That all depends on your staying silent," Jorge interrupts.

"Agreed. Secondly, I want you to anonymously pay the Coalition for Immigrants' Rights one million dollars. And I want Todd to pay Felicia a separation settlement of one hundred thousand dollars. In return I will give you all the cards I copied."

"If I do as you ask, how will I know you haven't made a second set of copies?" He's fast.

"If another copy became public, my life wouldn't be worth a dime, would it?"

"No. And it wouldn't be a fast death either."

"I'm not going to commit suicide to make a political point," I say. He stays silent, thinking. "So, do we have a deal?" I ask.

"I need to talk to the Grangers. You stay here."

Jorge leaves the room, locking the door from the outside. Hardly necessary, I reflect; I'd have to be crazy to attempt an escape. Now that the immediate threat has receded, my body starts shaking violently all over. I'm sweating from head to toe. My mouth is dry. I want to bawl my eyes out. But I know I have to be outwardly in control when Jorge returns.

Five minutes later Jorge enters with a check in his hand.

"Here," he says roughly, thrusting it at me, "this is Todd's check for Felicia."

Faking calm, I glance at the check in my hand and see that it is made out to Felicia for the right amount. Carefully, I slip it into my jeans pocket.

Jorge continues, "Todd says you are never to come back here."

I nod. "Of course."

"The Coalition for Immigrant Rights will receive an electronic transfer deposit of the million immediately after you give me the cards."

My mind scrambles, trying to figure out how to avoid being hoodwinked in the exchange. "Who will be meeting me?"

"I will," Jorge says.

"Okay." I pause to think. "I'll meet you tomorrow morning at 9 on the central steps outside the Federal Building on Wilshire." There are always guards outside the entrance. I can ask them to keep an eye on me when I meet up with Jorge, thereby minimizing my chances of being kidnapped. "I'll show you the cards. Then, once I see on my app that the funds have been transferred I'll hand the cards to you."

"I warn you," Jorge says, "I will have backup. So, no funny business with the Feds."

"As I said, I value my life too much."

"You'd better hurry if you want to make it by 8," Jorge says dismissively.

"See you tomorrow," I say and walk out of the open door without looking back, out into the cool evening air. I breathe in deeply, forcing myself to swallow the bile in my throat. My legs are so weak, I can barely walk. And I badly need to pee. But at this moment I can't think about anything but getting out of here as quickly as I can.

On my way to the 55 freeway I turn off at 18th Street and park. I look around to make sure I'm not being followed. The street looks deserted. I pull out my phone and dial Eduardo's number.

"Are you okay?" he asks anxiously. "How did it go?"

I tell him what happened, omitting the threats of violence.

"So," I conclude, "the Coalition is about to receive a major check."

"That's incredible. I can't thank you enough, Jenny. It's going to make a huge difference in what we can get done there. But I'm really concerned about your safety when you exchange the cards."

He cares, I think. Even while I am still shaky with fear, I am aware of how good that makes me feel. "I'm on my way," I tell him. "We can talk about that when I reach your place."

As I ease my way onto the freeway, I reflect on the side of myself that I just discovered. I stood up to three very powerful men and held my own. I made them compensate one of their victims and contribute to an organization that helps the people they make a profit from smuggling into the US. I may be in a big mess with no job or place of my own, but at least I took a stand. Let the world of money go its own way. I don't have to live my life by its standards. Money may matter. But so does self-respect, and so do personal relationships.

I turn on my car radio.

"Scandal-plagued Bell City Council will meet to schedule a recall election. Angry residents hope to vote the council out of office. Some seventy-five residents are lined up outside the council chambers tonight waiting to be admitted to the meeting . . ." Enough of corrupt politicians for one night.

I switch channels. Great! Rihanna is a short way into singing "Only Girl (In the World)." One line in the song catches my attention: "I'm the only one in command." I'm not convinced that's what I want in a new relationship, but I sure don't want to enter another unequal one. I hope I remember that, when the time comes. I drive on through the dark, happy to leave it to my GPS to direct me to Eduardo in Boyle Heights.

*

Eduardo's modest Craftsman Bungalow looks at least a hundred years old, set on an open stretch of stubble grass. Before I can knock, Eduardo flings the door open, pulls me inside, and holds me in a long, warm hug.

The living room walls are lined with books. To my right is a fireplace, topped by a Cinco de Mayo poster featuring a colorful Aztec warrior. The room is sparsely furnished with a leather sofa and matching armchair, a polished wooden coffee table, and a Spanish-style sideboard. The hardwood floor is covered with Mexican and Navajo rugs. At the back I can glimpse an open space leading to the kitchen with its stained pine cabinets.

Eduardo motions me to the sofa, into which I sink gratefully. Across from us on the coffee table are two wine glasses, an open bottle of Rioja, a basket of blue corn chips, and a bowl of green salsa. He sits next to me and pours us each a glass of the deep red wine.

"I can't tell you how worried I was," he says. "You don't know the Cartel the way I do, how ruthless it is. And I'm really impressed with the way you gave yourself an out."

I laugh. "Yes. I was patting myself on the back for that on the way here. Prepared and reckless at the same time. It's a new me."

"I liked the old one well enough."

"I was tired of her. She was too skillful at getting by."

"Getting by can be useful."

"It's also a great way to avoid taking control of your life. The new me is going to make my own decisions. Not just react to others."

"Let's drink to that," Laughing together, we clink glasses.

He turns to me and says in a different voice, "I've been wanting to tell you how much I love the color of your eyes. They're so luminous, like translucent pools."

The new me replies in kind. "And yours are gray and they glitter."

We're mesmerized, staring into each other's eyes. Then his phone rings.

"Damn," Eduardo curses. He looks at the caller ID and frowns.

He stands up. "Yes. What is it?"

After listening for a moment he says, "That would not be convenient at the moment."

I hear a woman's voice on the other end shouting.

"Help yourself," he says to me in a stage whisper, gesturing at the chips.

"Who're you talking to?" I hear the voice demand.

"No one. As for the payments, that was all settled back in August," Eduardo says firmly.

More shouting from the caller. "I'm not raising the amount," Eduardo repeats. "You'd only ask for more again."

The woman is now screaming at him, though I cannot make out what she's saying because Eduardo is slowly walking toward the kitchen.

He cuts her off. "A new TV? Are you kidding me? Get real, will you. I don't even have a TV. And you want me to buy you a new one? No way. I'm ending this conversation right now." He slams shut his phone.

After ending the call he walks back into the living room and puts his phone on the coffee table. As he sinks back into the sofa the phone starts ringing again. He reaches over and turns it off. I look at him quizzically.

"I'm really sorry. I was going to tell you . . ."

"You don't have to if you don't want to," I tell him. But I don't mean it, and he knows it.

"I think I do have to explain that call to you."

Nursing my warming glass of wine, I settle back against the arm of the sofa so that I can read his face as he continues.

"That was Isabella. We were together for a few months before we split up a year and a half ago. It was my doing. I should never have let myself get into that relationship. She was too needy and possessive. She was always asking me where I'd been and whom I'd been talking to. Then ten months after we had split up, Isabella told me that she'd had a baby the previous December and that it had to be mine."

Here we go, I think. So much for the Hollywood romantic ending. No walking hand in hand into the sunset. Strangely, my new self feels relieved at this.

He pauses for a sip of wine.

"Why didn't she tell you when she was pregnant?" I ask.

"Nothing about her is straightforward," Eduardo sighs. "I offered to pay her maintenance for Camila. Instead she took me to family court. She thought she could get more money from me that way. They offered her less than what I'd offered. She's still convinced that the court cheated her out of her rightful support."

"How do you know you're the father?" I ask.

A painful look crosses his face. "I'm pretty sure. She says she hasn't been with anyone else since we were together." Eduardo sighs. "I believe her, because she's still obsessed with me. But we are no good for one another. Of course, she refuses to see that."

"You mean she still wants to be with you?"

"Nothing I say or do seems to convince her that it's over. The worst thing is, I have to see her every time I see Camila, and every time I visit them she makes a play for me. She simply won't let go."

"Maybe you still find her attractive, and she senses that?" I ask.

Eduardo shakes his head. "All I think about when I am with her and Camila is how soon I can leave. I only go because I want to see how Camila is doing and hold her in my arms. She's a really sweet baby." He reaches for his cell phone and shows me a photo of a beautiful baby girl cradled in the arms of her mother. I note that Isabella is an attractive Latina in her mid-twenties with long black curly hair.

He pours us more wine and pushes the chips and salsa toward me. I decline. Why am I so disturbed? Eduardo and I barely know each other. Sure, I like him. I don't feel any jealousy about Isabella, but the thought that he already has a daughter disturbs me. He'll always be involved in a life that predates my knowing him. He'll always have to talk to and negotiate with Isabella about Camila. Isabella will always be a problem. If he and I have a relationship will Isabella finally give up on him? Or will she just blame me for his failure to return to her? It all seems so complicated.

I need to get a grip. I raise my glass to my lips and drink.

Eduardo can see that I'm confused. "I realize this must be a bit of a shock for you. I'm so sorry. I wanted to have one uncomplicated evening with you before filling you in on my messy past."

I rally. "You know what? We can do that. We don't have to be responsible tonight. Let's just postpone dealing with all this for now. I feel really hungry. Is there somewhere we can go for a meal?"

Eduardo grins. "You bet there is. Do you like mole?"

I nod.

"The best Pueblan mole in town is about ten minutes' walk from here. You can try out samples of their three kinds—almond, chipotle, and regular. Then choose what to have it with—tacos, enchiladas, chilaquiles. And the tortillas are handmade, not warmed up ready-mades."

"I'm ready to go right now," I say standing up.

*

When we get back from the restaurant a young woman is waiting for us on his front porch.

"I knew you were with some libertina when I called," she shouts when she sees us. "Does she know you're a father who has abandoned his baby daughter?"

We both stop in the front yard.

"Isabella, have you now taken to stalking me?" Eduardo asks sarcastically.

"You're a goddamn father. What are you doing hanging around with this perra?"

"Stop insulting someone you know nothing about."

"I don't need to know anything about this piece of scum. Clearly she's about to spend the night with you."

"That's none of your business."

"Of course it's my business. You should be at home with your daughter."

"This is my home, and, as you know, the custody order allows me to visit Camila only once every two weeks. So what are you talking about?"

"You always sound so reasonable, when in fact you're full of shit."

"I'm not going to stand out here arguing with you. Go home." He pauses, then asks, "Who's looking after Camila?"

"None of your business."

"If you've left her alone, it most certainly is."

"Keep your nose out of my life."

"You've just demanded that I do the opposite."

"Shut your mouth," she screams. "You think you're so smart. But you're a piece of shit."

"If you don't leave, I'm calling the cops," Eduardo says.

"Don't worry. I'm leaving you with your new puta," she yells. She runs down the steps, still shouting insults until she disappears around the corner. Some of the neighbors are watching through their doors and windows. I feel ashamed, as if I really am the loose other woman Isabella made me out to be.

Eduardo lets me into the house. We are both shaken by the encounter. He pours the rest of the Rioja into our glasses and sinks into the sofa.

"I think I ought to be going," I say.

"And where would you go?" he asks.

"There's always my parents' place."

"I'm not going to let Isabella ruin our first evening together."

His persistence wins me over. "I'm sorry," I say. "Isabella made me feel bad. I shouldn't let her do that. And I won't." I raise my glass and clink it with his.

Eduardo smiles. "She's just trying to make me look like a jerk to the neighbors. But they all know about her. It's not as if I bring women back here all the time. In fact, you are the first woman I've brought home since I broke up with Isabella."

"I would be flattered if I weren't pressuring you to help me out of a tight spot."

"If only you knew how much I want you to stay," he says. He takes hold of both my hands and presses them to his lips.

I use my captive hands to pull him towards me. Eduardo starts kissing me on the mouth, first with short urgent kisses, then with more lingering softer kisses that make me want to melt my whole body into him. He explores the inside of my mouth with his tongue, tentatively feeling his way round and under my tongue. I reciprocate, and we end up with dueling tongues that make us break apart to burst out laughing at each other.

He stands and holds out his hands to help me up. Still facing me, he draws me with him as he walks backwards to the bedroom. We stop in the doorway to embrace. His hands explore my back, my ass, the backs of my thighs. He presses his erection into my belly. I slide my hands round from his back to grasp his penis through his trousers. He moans with desire. "I am going to make you moan a lot louder and longer," I tell him as I very slowly rub him up and down.

He pulls my blouse over my head as I undo the buttons of his shirt and peel it off him. His chest is hairless, his skin taut. He unhooks my bra and sinks his face into my breasts.

"Your skin is so soft and tender," he murmurs as he grasps my breasts in both hands.

I caress his back and grasp his buttocks. "God, I want you all at once, and I don't want it ever to be over," I tell him as I slide one hand between his legs to grasp his testicles. I undo his belt and zipper and help him step out of his jeans. We do the same with my jeans and thong.

I take him by the hands and pull him down with me onto the bed. He is kissing my forehead, pausing to savor my lips, pausing again to lick my belly button, then working his way further down my body slowly, slowly until I can feel his tongue between my legs, exploring the contours of my interior. Now he's found the spot.

Ohhh! Now it's my turn to let out a low cry of pleasure. "I want you so badly," he whispers in my ear, "I want you just as much," I say, guiding his erect penis up into me. He rolls on top of me, but, after gripping him around the waist with my legs, I roll us back to a side-by-side position. We both begin to move together side to side, backwards and forwards, in and out.

He stops. "I need a condom," he says, reaching into the bedside cabinet.

Quickly we return to our intoxicating rhythmic movement. We are a single body riding the waves of desire. The rest of the world doesn't exist. I am all body and no body. I'm weightless. We occupy a state of sheer need. The rocking of our bodies picks up speed and urgency, and our breathing becomes louder as we encourage each other to abandon all restraint and give ourselves over to the overpowering desire to reach our climax.

I feel exhausted and excited and absurdly happy. We roll onto our backs. "Again, but later," Eduardo murmurs and falls fast asleep. In seconds I do the same.

MIGUEL

Miguel wakes up from a deep sleep and finds himself in his cell bed. In his dream he was on his honeymoon with Adela. They were strolling along a deserted beach in Oahu as a blood-red sun was sinking into the dark blue-black ocean.

A guard is shaking him.

"Wake up!" he's saying loudly. "Your transport is here."

"What time is it?" Miguel asks.

"What's it to you?" the guard jeers.

Miguel looks at his watch. It's 3:05 am.

"You're being taken to El Centro for processing. Get up and follow me."

Miguel is still wearing the clothes he was arrested in. He rolls up his blanket, collects his toiletries, and follows the guard to a sterile, empty room. Another guard—large, heavy, tanned, with a tattoo on his bare right arm shoves a pile of paperwork at Miguel and tells him to sign where indicated.

Miguel feels uncomfortable under his gaze. There is something weird about the way the guy is eyeing him, as if he were sizing up a horse at an auction.

Once the paperwork is all signed, the guard handcuffs him and shackles his ankles. Miguel feels like a trussed-up chicken at Cal Fowl.

"Follow me!" the guard commands.

Miguel shuffles along a corridor, shackles clanging, up a flight of stairs, one awkward step at a time, and through a metal door into a closed courtyard where a black van is waiting with its rear doors open. The guard shoves Miguel roughly into the van, follows him inside, and locks him in the cage inside. The van's doors slam shut, and the van takes off, throwing him against the metal mesh walls of the cage. "Stupid jerk!" Miguel swears as he wedges himself into a seated position against the bars.

About an hour later the van stops. The rear doors are flung open from the outside.

Miguel peers into the darkness and sees only a dirt road and the shadows of trees. The guard enters and unlocks the cage door.

"What's happening?" Miguel asks.

"Get out!" the guard says.

"Where are we?" Miguel asks, not moving.

"None of your business!" the guard shouts.

"Why do you want me to get out in this godforsaken place?"

"So we can have a little fun together."

Miguel's heart pounds. "What kind of fun?" he stalls.

"Come on. You know what I mean."

"I'm not gay, if that is what you're thinking," Miguel says indignantly.

"Neither am I," he replies. "But I never miss out on a bit of fun."

"I'm not leaving the van."

There is a pause. Then the guard shouts angrily at Miguel, "What a loser. You're going to pay for this."

The guard locks the cage door shut, slams the van doors, and drives off at a speed that throws Miguel against the gate of the cage. For the rest of the trip the driver alternates emergency stops with screeching, sharp turns. Miguel tries to jam himself between the bars but is repeatedly sent crashing to the other side of the cage. All he can do is curse loudly, undoubtedly giving the guard pleasure, if not the kind of pleasure he had in mind.

*

Miguel lies in his bunk bed in a dorm alongside fifty other male detainees at El Centro Detention Facility, fifteen miles from the border at Mexicali. There is no air-conditioning, and the heat is already oppressive.

When he was delivered here while it was still dark he was treated like some criminal—questioned, photographed, fingerprinted, stripped naked, and issued two pairs of one-size underwear, socks, shoes, shower shoes, a shirt, and pants. He was allowed to keep only $40 in cash and two photos, one of his parents and one of Adela showing a lot of cleavage.

"Get an eyeful of this," one of the guards called out to his coworker. "She looks ready for it, don't she?" When Miguel angrily told the guard to give him back the photo, the guard shouted back at him, "When you address uniformed staff, you refer to us by rank and last name. Officer Wright in my case."

"Whatever," Miguel muttered angrily.

"Say it now."

"Okay, Officer Wright."

"That's better."

The rest of Miguel's possessions, including his credit card, driver's license, door keys, pen, phone, and clothes, were "retained for safekeeping." All he got was an itemized list of them. When he asked to take a shower the guard snapped at him that if he stopped making demands he might be allowed a shower after his recreation period. After attaching a red wristband to him, the guard ushered him into the dorm, assigned him a bed, and told him to undress and lie down until lights on at 5:30 am.

Miguel is awakened by a loud buzzer that bores into his fearful dreams of being savaged by a cougar. The lights burst on. He has no idea how to conduct himself, so he decides to imitate whatever the other inmates do. Cursing and coughing, they begin dressing and making up their beds. Then they stand by their beds waiting—for what, Miguel doesn't know. Next, two guards appear and one of them shouts out, "Roll call. Everyone stand still! No talking!" The guards match each detainee against his photo ID. When they get to Miguel there are no papers.

"Name?" the guard asks Miguel.

"Miguel Mondragon."

"Miguel Mondragon, Officer," the guard yells in Miguel's face. "Try that again."

"Miguel Mondragon, Officer."

"There's no Miguel Mondragon on my roll," says the guard accusingly.

"That's not my fault," Miguel replies.

"Don't get smart with me," the guard shouts. "When did you arrive?"

"This morning."

"This morning, Officer."

"This morning, Officer."

"That motherfucking processor. It's not the first time he's screwed up," he says to the younger guard. "Go to Processing and tell them to give you his photo ID and papers. Double quick."

All the detainees are left standing in silence while Miguel's papers are fetched. It isn't his fault, but many of them look at Miguel resentfully. Great start, he thinks. There is a further delay while the guards wait to hear that all the counts in the other dorms have been completed.

Finally the detainees are marched to the cafeteria for breakfast. Miguel realizes that he's starving. But breakfast turns out to be a plastic tray with compartments for cream of wheat, which is cold with lumps in it, half a cup of diluted mixed fruit juice, a biscuit with "country gravy," and a cup of weak lukewarm coffee. Miguel is too depressed to care. Arturo, the guy who sleeps in the bed next to his and who has adopted Miguel, takes Miguel's biscuit, dips it into his milk (he knows better than to choose coffee), and swallows it with a satisfied smack of his lips.

A few hours later the inmates of Miguel's dorm are allowed an hour's recreation in the dirt yard, exposed to the blazing sun in the scorching desert heat. The detainees crouch together against the only wall offering shade, desperate for what little relief it offers, while the guards grin at them from their air-conditioned observation rooms. Like the others, Miguel is sweating profusely. After what seems like ages, the men are marched back to the dorm.

Twenty-four hours ago, Miguel reflects, I was with Adela talking about buying frozen yogurt at Pinkberry's. The thought of the cool treat entering his mouth only makes him feel hotter and more depressed. He curses himself for not putting his own safety first when those bastards from ICE started manhandling the young woman. His stand had not stopped them from arresting her. So what was the point of it? There was none. What a fool you are, he tells himself.

*

After the recreation period Miguel and the other detainees are marched back to the shower room. There everyone strips off their clothes and puts on shower shoes. Miguel's bunkmate, Arturo, signals Miguel to step into the shower next to him, separated by a divider extending from waist to knees.

Miguel tries to turn down the burning water, but the faucet doesn't move. The same proves true of the cold faucet. Arturo, observing him, shouts over the noise of running water that the temperature is controlled by the guards.

"Hot water makes me hot," he says.

Miguel looks questioningly at him.

"Sí. Look at me," Arturo says.

Miguel peers over the partition. Arturo has a massive hard-on.

"You want to help me?" Arturo grins.

"No way," Miguel responds.

"What if I help you?" Arturo's hand comes around the side and moves down towards Miguel's penis.

"I said 'No.'"

"Okay. Okay. But at least you can help me." He grabs hold of Miguel's wrist and pulls it towards his upright penis.

Where are the guards? Miguel asks himself.

"Stop it!" Miguel shouts. "Let go of me."

The detainee showering on the other side of Miguel grins and says to Miguel, "That's what we do for each other. That's one of the few pleasures left to us. No mujeres. So stop making a fuss."

"Listen. I'm not jerking him off. No way."

"Maybe we stick this soap up your butt instead?"

"Leave me alone," Miguel is close to tears. "Just fucking leave me alone!"

A guard appears behind him.

"What you shouting for?" he asks.

"Why are you leaving me alone with a bunch of perverts?"

"What're you talking about? Who's a pervert?" asks the guard.

"All of you," Miguel shouts back in a temper.

"You calling me a pervert, you pathetic wetback?"

Arturo chimes in, "That's what he was yelling."

"Stay out of this, you."

The guard turns to Miguel.

"Time you learned some respect," he says.

"Bob!" he calls out to a fellow guard.

Bob slouches over from where he has been leaning against the doorjamb. "Yeah?"

"This jerk just called us all perverts."

"Sounds like he needs time out," Bob says.

"Just what I'm thinking," the first guard says. "Get your clothes on," he tells Miguel.

"But I'm not finished showering."

"Get your clothes on. Now!"

Miguel hastily rubs himself dry and dresses. Each guard grabs him by an arm. They frog-march him down a long hallway, out into the sweltering-hot yard, and into another cell block. They stop at a metal door with a small grated window in it and unlock the door. It is totally dark inside.

"What's going on?" Miguel asks.

"Nobody taught you to say 'Officer'?"

"What's going on, Officer?"

"That's better. We're saving you from all us perverts." Both guards chortle. "You don't have to worry about being abused in a hold cell."

The two of them shove Miguel into the cell and slam the door shut behind him.

Silence. Darkness. Miguel gropes his way around the cell. He stumbles into a bucket and knocks it over. Liquid swirls around his feet. He reaches out for the bucket and returns it to an upright position. His hands feel sticky. He continues his search and knocks his knee against something hard. After groping along its edge, he concludes it is some sort of bunkbed. He carefully lowers himself onto it and sinks his head into his hands.

"You fool!" Miguel curses himself. "You just can't keep your big mouth shut, can you? Once is not enough. When will you learn?"

The black silence offers no reply.

TUESDAY,
NOVEMBER 2, 2010

Eduardo insists on driving me to the Federal Building to deliver the cards. Eduardo turns on the car radio, and we hear Dan being interviewed by a female reporter from Fox News: "It breaks my heart," Dan is saying, "but Gomez deserved to be deported. The law's the law. He used a false social security number. He lied about his immigration status. It tears me up. At the same time, I don't believe the voters will be thinking about Gomez when they come to vote today. There are so many vital issues to be decided in this election."

"Please," I say to Eduardo, "can we not listen to that slime ball. How about some music?"

Eduardo changes channels to KUSC. The Morning Show is playing Vivaldi's *The Four Seasons* for what must be the hundredth time this year.

I think back to waking up in Eduardo's bed two hours ago, to the cup of coffee he brought me, to the sexy shower we took together, and to our dreamy breakfast at the kitchen table.

That idyll came to an abrupt end when I turned on my cell phone to check my email. The first message was from Dad, asking if I could get to their place by 3 for an urgent family conference. He'd already spoken to Tricia on the phone, he said, and she could make it then. What the hell is going on? I wondered. But there was no time to call Dad or Tricia before rushing to this morning's meeting with Jorge. I quickly emailed Dad saying I would be there, and texted Tricia to ask if she wanted to drive to the Valley together.

As Eduardo is parking in the public lot next to the Federal Building, he says, "I want to go with you to meet Jorge."

"No way," I say. "That's not the deal I made with him. What I do want you to do is position yourself near the guards at the entrance. If anything looks suspicious, you can ask them to intervene."

"Your call. But I don't want anything to happen to you now I'm finally getting to know you."

"Wait for me to text you that the wire transfer is going through. Once you've confirmed that the money has arrived, it should all be over."

We take off, Eduardo to a position near the guards, I to the side facing Veteran Avenue, as agreed with Jorge.

The wait seems forever. Finally, a black Lincoln Town Car pulls over to the curb, discharges Jorge and two other men, and speeds off. Jorge leaves the two others on the sidewalk and takes the path to where I'm waiting.

"You got the cards?" he says without preamble.

"Yes," I say.

"Show them to me—discreetly," he says.

I open the envelope and fan out the five cards inside it.

"That's all you have?" he asks.

I nod.

"I need to test one before we seal the deal," he says.

I hand him the card from the kitchen. He takes out a portable card player, inserts the card, and watches a few seconds of it.

"Let me see the others," he says, and holds out his hand.

"We agreed that you get those when the money has been transferred to the Coalition's account."

Jorge hesitates. It can't be often he accepts instructions from others. Nervous, I hold my breath.

"Okay," he says. "Wait while I make the transaction."

After a few moments he nods. "Done."

"Let me make sure the money's been received." I text Eduardo. Jorge and I stand there in silence. After a brief wait Eduardo's text comes through. "It's there."

"Okay," I tell Jorge. As prearranged, Eduardo will have already changed the password for the Coalition's account, to avoid further access to it.

"Now give me the envelope. And remember," Jorge says menacingly, "if anything about this deal ever becomes public, we will hunt you down and make you pay a terrible price. Got it?"

"Yes. Don't worry. I value my life."

I hand him the envelope. "You think a million makes you a winner?" Jorge sneers. "You could have got a lot more, chica, if you knew how to play this game. A million! It's just loose change to us."

I take a step away from him, then turn back. "One final question. Is Susan still alive?"

"Shall we say her body will never be found?"

My heart sinks. "You bastards."

Jorge shrugs, unmoved. We take off in different directions. It's over.

*

Eduardo drives us to Gloria's apartment so that I can tell Felicia that she's free as well as cash-rich. I tell Eduardo what Jorge told me about Susan. He looks shocked. "How terrible," he says. "Were you close to her?"

"Not really, but Felicia was, and I don't know how I'm going to break the news to her."

As we park in front of Gloria's, the neighborhood kid is hanging in her doorway. Eduardo gives him a dollar and tells him to watch the car.

I've barely knocked on the door when Felicia throws it open. She hugs me with tears in her eyes. Eduardo and Gloria watch us indulgently.

"What news?" she asks anxiously.

"For a start, you're in the clear."

Felicia looks confused. "In the clear?"

"You are no longer in danger. The cartel is no longer trying to get you out of the country."

"Why no longer?" Felicia asks, looking befuddled.

"Because Todd canceled his deal with the cartel."

Obviously I am not explaining myself clearly, as she asks me, "Why Mr. Granger change his mind?"

"Because I came to an arrangement with him. In return for giving him the recordings that tie him and Dan to the cartel's money, he agreed to call off the cartel and give you a check for $100,000 as compensation."

"$100,000!" Felicia is shocked.

"In return for complete silence about the recordings and your illegal status."

"That is easy. Hardly worth $100,000."

"You bet it's worth that," I assure her. "If the press caught wind of that, Dan's career would be over, and Todd would be facing prosecution for money laundering."

"Still. Is mucho dinero."

"And what do you think your long service to him is worth?"

Felicia shrugs. We are silent for a moment. I reflect how tough it is going to be for Felicia to find another job with no reference.

Then she asks anxiously, "What has happened to Miguel?"

"We don't know for sure. But it is very likely that he has been deported to Mexico by now."

"Pobrecito!" Felicia moans.

"We couldn't locate him in the system. And he'd already signed away his rights to a hearing in immigration court."

"I certain they threatened him. I know what they're like," she says.

"I'm sure you're right."

I dread telling her the next piece of news. I hesitate, then take the plunge. "I'm afraid I have more bad news."

Felicia stares at me fearfully.

"I just learned that the cartel murdered Susan."

Felicia lets out an animal-sounding howl. "But why?" she cries out.

"Because they were afraid she would tell Eduardo about the connection between the cartel, Todd, and Dan."

"She not harm anyone," Felicia sobs out. "So unfair."

"I know," I say tearfully, holding her in my arms.

I wait for her sobs to subside.

"At least you're no longer in danger. And here's the check from Todd." I fish it out of my purse and hand it to her.

Felicia stares at it in silent disbelief.

"You can go back home now," I say.

"Yes. I know," Felicia says. "I cannot wait to hold my poor husband in my arms. First his nephew is deported. Then his wife is missing. He even stopped eating. Juan not eating! Never has that happened before."

"I know you want to see him as soon as possible," I say. "But I would strongly urge you to first go to the bank and deposit that check. Just in case."

"But poor Susan," Felicia says. "I'll miss her muchisimo."

"I know," I sympathize. "So brutal. I thought we should have a small memorial ceremony for her tomorrow morning. Just the three of us. Sort of lay her spirit to rest."

"Please. Yes."

"How about if we pick you up at ten?"

"Ten good. Thank you so much, Jenny. For everything."

"Let me call a taxi for you," says Eduardo.

"Gracias. Gracias a todos. You both help me so much."

"You didn't deserve this," I tell Felicia as we leave the apartment. "And you do deserve the check."

*

By 2:30 that afternoon I'm in Tricia's new red Corvette Z06 en route to our parents' house in the Valley. She's a manic driver, weaving in and out of the lanes, and entering and exiting the diamond lane if that puts her a car's length ahead.

When I got to her apartment she had stacked my belongings in the hallway, more than ready to be rid of me. We never did have much affection for one another. She was always ultracompetitive— valedictorian, summa cum laude, rich boyfriends, high paying job, designer clothes. We just couldn't be more different.

We had time to walk together to our local polling station at the Westminster Senior Center in Venice. We voted in adjacent booths, a somewhat futile exercise for both of us since we canceled out each other's votes. I voted for Brown, she for Granger. I voted for Boxer, she for Fiorina. I voted the Democratic Party slate, she the Republican. Standing next to her, separated by just a canvas screen, dramatized our adversarial relationship.

"So where did you sleep last night?" she asks me as we drive to the Valley.

"At Eduardo's," I say neutrally.

"Too bad," she comments.

"What do you mean?"

"It's a romantic thing, right?"

"You could call it that," I say guardedly.

"That's what you do when you're in your teens."

"What is?"

"Give it away for nothing."

"If you love someone you will give them anything," I say and immediately regret letting slip the word, "love."

"So, we're in love now. And with a Mexican American?"

"So?"

"When I was nineteen I had a hot affair with a guy from Guadalajara. He was incredibly good looking and amazing in bed. Then one day he just disappeared from my life. When I tried locating him, I found that he'd left his job and moved out of his apartment at night without paying that month's rent. The cab company he worked for told me he'd given notice at the end of the previous month. So it was all planned in advance. But not a word to me."

"Why do you think that was?"

"A close friend of his told me that ICE was closing in on him. He was due to make a court appearance the day he vanished."

"So that's why you no longer give it away for nothing?"

"No. That's why I don't trust Mexicans."

"Eduardo isn't Mexican."

"You're playing with words. He even makes his living defending Mexican illegals."

"You mean with undocumented immigrants, not all of whom are Mexican?"

"Now you're quibbling with words again."

"No, I'm not. Eduardo is an American citizen. He's as American as you or I."

"I don't trust them."

"And whom do you mean by 'them'?"

"Latinos. They have different values than ours. Different loyalties. Different attitudes toward women too."

"You know, you sound horribly racist," I say, looking round at her. She's not used to being confronted by me. I usually shrug off or ignore her attacks and innuendos. But confronting her is the new me.

"You need to start living in the real world. A lot of Americans think the way I do. They just keep quiet about it when they're with liberal types like you."

"I'm sure you're right. Dan Granger has been spouting those prejudiced opinions out loud throughout the campaign."

"Exactly. We're transitioning to an age where political correctness is losing ground to gut feelings."

"That's where you're wrong. My gut feelings totally coincide with what you call political correctness."

"Oh, you! You just think you're in love. How sad that you've chosen another outsider."

"You don't know Eduardo. So please stop making judgments based on your ignorance."

"I know his type well enough. That's enough for me."

"Okay. This conversation is over. Got it?"

Inevitably she has to have the last word. "You'll see that I'm right sooner or later."

I go silent. To have a bigot for a sister is so humiliating. Where did she get it? Certainly not from our liberal parents. The people in the wealthy crowd she hangs with have a thing up their collective butt about immigrants—about anyone who isn't like them—blacks, Asians, the poor, the mentally ill . . .

After a few minutes Tricia pulls out of her purse a Ziploc and extracts some blue pills.

"Want one?" she says to me.

"Those barbs?" I ask.

"That's right."

"No thanks."

"I just can't face Mother and Father without a little assistance."

Tricia slips a pill into her mouth and washes it down with bottled water.

"That was Gary's regular excuse whenever he took one," I say.

"Gary!" Tricia snorts. After a pause she remarks, "You know that for the last three years he has been my main supplier?"

"Gary dealt drugs?" I ask incredulously.

"Sure. How do you think he made his money?"

"Why didn't you tell me this before?"

"I didn't want to risk my supply chain."

"What do you mean?"

"I thought you would get all ethical and interrupt my supply."

"So all the time you were ridiculing Gary to my face you were relying on him to feed your addiction."

"What's wrong with that? That's all he was good for. A not very reliable messenger boy."

"You're unbelievable."

"He's a sleaze ball. He even tried coming on to me on one occasion. Wanted sex instead of payment."

"And?"

"What do you think? A year's worth of drugs wouldn't have bought him even a hand job."

I'm left speechless. Over the last few days so many people I thought I knew have revealed a darker, more sordid side. Did I deliberately blind myself to this harsher reality?

My thoughts are interrupted by our arrival at our parents' house.

*

Dad seats the four of us at the dining room table. Mom doesn't look well. She's avoiding looking at any of us.

Dad clears his throat. "We've been keeping this to ourselves for some time now, but it's time for us to talk about it." He pauses and takes a gulp of water. "Your mother has been diagnosed with vascular dementia."

"What's that exactly?" Tricia asks.

"It's a form of dementia caused by multiple strokes and lesions to blood vessels in the brain."

So, that explains her erratic behavior, I think. Preoccupied with my own mounting problems, I have ignored her frequent memory lapses, refusing to face the obvious. Now that her dementia is confirmed I allow myself to experience the shock I have repressed until this moment.

"And how long has this been going on?" Tricia asks.

"This particular condition is very hard to diagnose. Over the last year she has undergone numerous tests—blood tests of every variety, X-rays, ECGs, neuroimaging, and a wide number of cognitive tests. The definitive diagnosis was only confirmed yesterday."

"And why haven't you told us about this all that time?" Tricia demands.

"We didn't want to worry either of you, dear, until we knew," Dad answers.

"It's a lot of nonsense," Mom says to the glass of water in front of her.

"Your mother refuses to admit that there's anything wrong with her, apart from a little depression." Dad says.

She looks up at him angrily. "That's because there isn't."

"What about you getting lost in the bathroom this morning?" he asks her gently.

"That was just for a moment," she says.

"Alright. What day is it today?" he asks patiently.

"How should I know?" she replies, flustered. "He's always trying to trap me like that," she says to Tricia and me.

"Or how about your setting the microwave on fire on Saturday by setting it to heat up a frozen bagel for thirty minutes?"

"I set it for three minutes. You just won't believe me."

Dad addresses us. "It's getting too dangerous to leave her on her own when I go to work. She gets dizzy spells on the staircase. She leaves the front door wide open when she goes out. She turns the burner on and walks away. She forgets to eat when she's on her own—"

"It's not my fault," she shouts. "I leave myself a note of what there is for lunch, and then I lose the note."

Dad sadly shrugs his shoulders at us, as if to say, "You see?"

"So," says Tricia, "what do the doctors recommend?"

"They want me to go live in one of those terrible places," Mom says.

Dad nods. "They strongly urge me to find her a place in an assisted living facility."

"So?" Tricia asks her father.

"I was told what the diagnosis was likely to be months ago. I've been researching assisted living facilities in the Valley. The best one is called Encino Senior Living. It's on Ventura Boulevard. Here's their brochure."

Dad pushes the glossy booklet across the table to us. On the cover is a courtyard furnished with flowers and shrubs, deck tables, cushioned outdoor chairs, a glassed-in gazebo—and no humans. "Located in tree-lined Encino, this prime location offers healthcare facilities and providers, as well as places of worship, restaurants, and a nearby shopping center and entertainment complex . . . Patients suffering from Alzheimer's disease and dementia are offered individualized mental exercises encompassing the six areas of cognition . . ."

"How much does this cost?" asks Tricia, the practical one.

"Your mother has a modest life insurance policy that can be converted to pay the facility directly."

"For how long?" Tricia asks.

"Five-and-a-half years."

"And after that?" Tricia presses him.

Mom interrupts. "Don't worry about that. According to the doctors I only have four years maximum left."

I am stunned. I had never faced the obvious fact that my parents wouldn't be around for the rest of my life. They were a fixture in my mind. I feel sort of uprooted.

Dad looks kind of defeated.

"When is she moving in?" Tricia asks coldly, as if she were negotiating with one of her clients.

"Tomorrow," Dad says with a quiver in his voice. I reach out and touch his arm.

Tricia pulls out a checkbook and writes a check. Looking over her shoulder, I see the amount: one thousand dollars. She hands it to Mom.

"You always were generous," Mom says.

I feel a stab of envy. Mom never could say that to me. All I can offer her is love.

"When are visiting hours?" I ask.

"Pretty much any time apart from mealtimes and medical sessions," Dad answers.

"I'll visit you as soon as you're settled in," I tell Mom.

"Settled in," she replies with a snort. "That's a joke."

"I'm sorry," says Tricia, "but I have to get back to a client by 4." She looks at me. "We need to leave now."

"I'll phone you tomorrow, Dad," I say. "You and I can visit Mom together after you get back from work." I pull back my chair reluctantly and get up.

"Thanks, both of you," Dad says.

"Surprise! I've got news for you. I'm going to live in an assaulted living facility," Mom calls out as Tricia and I are walking away.

Eduardo and I are celebrating at Tlapazola, a gourmet Mexican restaurant on Venice Boulevard. When I protested that I couldn't afford it, he told me not to let a small thing like money stop us from savoring a victory. Besides, he's treating tonight.

We are on our second margarita. Our entrées have already arrived—Wild Lobster Tail Vegetable Enchiladas for Eduardo, and Black Tiger Shrimp Fajitas for me.

"Fantastic," I declare, wiping my lips with my napkin.

"I agree."

The waiter asks if we want dessert or coffee. We order two espressos. As we sip them, Eduardo leans across the table and says in a low voice, "I am having real difficulty staying on this side of the table."

"Greedy," I tease him.

"I feel as if I'm in a force field."

"So now we're blaming physics, are we?"

He grins. "All I know is that if we don't get you back to my place quickly I am going to get arrested for lewd conduct in public."

"We can't have that," I say. "Drink up, and let's get out of here."

On the car ride home we make the mistake of listening to the news on NPR: "Just minutes ago the polls closed on the West Coast. Republicans have made big gains nationwide and are projected to take over the House and sweep into a majority of governors' mansions."

We exchange a glum look. "We're projecting wins for Democrats Jerry Brown for governor and Barbara Boxer for the Senate in California." Eduardo and I exchange a high five. That news frees us from our obsession with the election, so we can devote the rest of the evening to each other.

MIGUEL

It is 8 in the morning. Miguel stands alone in the Oaxaca airport. When he was released, the guards told him that he was getting "deep repatriation." No driving over the border for him. Flown in handcuffs in a plane contracted by ICE, he has been returned to the city where he was born twenty years ago. His first memories are of his childhood in Baldwin Park. He has never visited Mexico. Never dared risk it. Now here he is back in a birthplace that he cannot even recall.

The grandly named Xoxocotlan International Airport turns out to be a single terminal with three gates. Miguel has no idea what "Xoxocotlan" means or what language it belongs to. Passengers' voices bounce off the hard surfaces of the building. Announcements over the PA are totally distorted and must be shouted out again in person by uniformed personnel.

Miguel exchanges the few dollars he had when he was arrested for pesos. Next he finds a public phone, consults the phone book to find the number of his grandparents, and dials that number.

"Bueno!" says a male voice.

Miguel knows only a few words of Spanish.

"Con—mm—quién hablo?"

"Miguel! Su padre llamó . . ." The rest was drowned by a PA announcement.

"I can't hear you. Damn! No puedo—what's the Spanish for 'hear'?"

"Qué estás diciendo?" asks the male voice on the phone.

Miguel looks round him in desperation. An older woman waiting for the phone offers to help. "'No te puedo oír' means 'I cannot hear you,'" she tells Miguel. He repeats this into the phone. His grandfather, presumably, replies with the same sentence about his father doing or saying something.

Still unable to understand him, Miguel turns to the woman behind him and holds out the phone. "I think my grandfather is trying to tell me something about my father, but I don't know enough Spanish to understand what he's saying. Could you please explain the situation to him?" She nods and speaks in Spanish with his grandfather.

She turns to Miguel. "Your grandfather was phoned by your father last night and told that you might be deported anytime. He wants you to take the shuttle to the Zócalo."

"What's the Zócalo?" Miguel asks her.

"The central square," she tells him.

"Oh. Please tell my grandfather that I'll do as he asks and meet him there. Could you also describe to him what I look like?"

The woman nods, talks some more into the phone and hangs up. Miguel thanks her and asks her where he can pick up the shuttle.

Following her instructions, Miguel makes his way out of the terminal, buys a ticket, and joins the line awaiting the arrival of the bus.

The drive to the city center takes him through some flat green farmland ringed by wooded mountains. They stop in the center of San Antonio de la Cal, and street vendors scramble on board to try to sell their wares during the five-minute layover.

The bus rolls through the suburbs of Oaxaca, streets of row houses painted in different colors, with broad, brightly painted window frames and tall doors with decorated porticos.

The Zócalo is an enormous tree-filled square humming with people, balloons, flowers, street cleaners, and vendors. Miguel gets off the shuttle and looks around for his grandfather. Most of the men he sees seem to be his grandfather's age.

Miguel dreads the moment he will have to try to talk to his grandfather. How will he survive here when he cannot speak the language? Will he be like Mexicans at home, who don't know any English and therefore must accept the lowest-paid and most unpleasant jobs?

Miguel catches sight of an old man walking toward him with a slight limp. This must be his grandfather; he's smiling and waving his arms. He's a short man with white bristles on his chin, a tanned leathery face, and a missing upper front tooth. He's carrying a plastic bag filled with fruit and vegetables.

"Hola, Miguel!" he shouts.

Miguel manages one of his few Spanish phrases: "Mucho gusto."

His grandfather reaches up to embrace him with both arms and slaps his back repeatedly. Finally he breaks away, launching into a long speech unintelligible to Miguel. What should Miguel call this stranger? He cannot recall the Spanish for grandfather. So he just nods and says "Sí. Sí."

Eventually he gathers from gestures that his grandfather wants him to walk with him. For the next thirty minutes, as they walk, his grandfather chatters. Miguel nods away and adds a "Sí" whenever it seems appropriate. Miguel is utterly miserable, doubly estranged by geography and language.

Finally, the two of them reach a street of brightly colored row houses. Outside an orange stucco single-story house a group of women and children are waving at them. Miguel waves back awkwardly, aware that in a few more moments they will learn how little Spanish he speaks. Before he knows it he is enveloped in hugs and kisses accompanied by greetings that he longs to understand.

A young girl of about twelve is urged to the front of the group. Shyly, she tells Miguel, "I speak small English."

"Thank you," Miguel says. "What's your name?"

"Teresa," she says. "I am your cousin."

"Please tell everyone I'm grateful for their wonderful welcome," Miguel says. As Teresa translates this, they respond with dismissive gestures, as if to ask, where else could they be when a relative from abroad arrives?

A wizened elderly woman dressed in black addresses him. He turns to Teresa for a translation.

"Your abuela—how to say it? —"

"My grandmother?" Miguel guesses.

"Sí, your grandmother asks you inside. She gives breakfast."

"Muchas gracias," Miguel says to his grandmother.

"Ven, mi nieto," she responds, grasping his arm and shepherding him through the open door.

The living room is dominated by a large painted wooden table and upright wooden chairs. The yellow ochre walls are hung with decorated crosses, pictures of the Virgin, masks, and hand-painted plates. A worn plastic fan slowly whirs on the tiled ledge in the corner. The floor is paved with Saltillo tiles. A light bulb covered with a paper shade hangs over the table. Two windows, one each side of the door, offer some additional light.

One place at the head of the table has been laid for Miguel. The women and his grandfather seat themselves around the table; the children stare at him from their places between their mothers and aunts.

Miguel's grandmother pours him out a cup of dark coffee from a hand-painted ceramic pot. "Yo sé que a los americanos les encanta su café," she tells the others. Miguel grins uncomprehendingly. Another woman emerges from the kitchen and sets a platter in front of him. On it is a huge yellow omelet covered with red salsa, green chili peppers, chorizos, and slices of avocado, accompanied by a basket of corn tortillas covered with a colorful woven cloth.

"Que aproveche!" she says.

"Muchas gracias," Miguel replies. Overwhelmed, he grasps a fork, looks down at his breakfast, looks up at all of them, and bursts into tears.

WEDNESDAY,
NOVEMBER 3, 2010

E duardo, Felicia, and I are standing on the beach at the edge of the Pacific Ocean. Each of us holds a white rose in our hands. We're here to say goodbye to Susan by recalling our chosen memory of her.

Felicia remembers the time her car broke down and she'd had it towed to Todd's driveway. Susan asked for the keys. At the end of the day she told Felicia that her car was working and gave her back the keys. When Felicia asked her how that could be, Susan told her that she'd asked a mechanic friend of hers to look at it. Days later Felicia came across a bill Susan had accidentally left in the kitchen. It revealed that Susan had paid a Newport Beach repair shop $2,800 to fix it.

When Felicia told her she wanted to pay her back, Susan just gave her a big hug and refused to discuss it.

Eduardo remembers the time Susan was advising a young Mexican woman who was due to appear in immigration court the following day. The woman had paid a shyster immigration lawyer who had all her paperwork when he was arrested. Susan visited the lawyer in jail, shamed him into telling her where the young woman's papers were being held, and drove to a dingy office in San Bernardino, where she recovered the paperwork in time to submit it to the judge the following day.

I recall the time I managed to flood Todd's master bedroom carpet while watering a large potted Kentia Palm. The water stain was dark brown, and I thought I'd have to have it professionally cleaned or even replaced. Susan came to the rescue with pails of warm soapy water, an unending supply of towels, and a hair dryer that she locked in position with a giant clamp she found in the garage. Before Todd got home the stain was gone and the carpet dry.

Once we are done with our memories, we throw our roses into the ocean and watch them float away until their white shapes become indistinguishable from the white crests of the waves far out at sea.

*

Eduardo has taken the day off to spend it with me. We're having a leisurely lunch, reading today's *LA Times*. The headline reads:

"GOP SWEEPS HOUSE; BROWN WINS."

"The Republican wave crashing across the nation stopped at the California border on Tuesday, as Jerry Brown won the governorship and U.S. Sen. Barbara Boxer claimed a victory that would send her back to Washington for a fourth term."

Several paragraphs down, the article comes closer to home. "Granger spent much campaign time impugning welfare recipients and illegal immigrants. Granger's lack of a human touch was reinforced when his former handyman announced in a tear-strewn interview that the candidate had thrown him out 'like a piece of garbage' after he admitted that he was in the country illegally."

Eduardo looks up from his reading. "I want to talk to you about the future."

"You've been distracting me from that," I joke, "ever since I turned up on your doorstep—when was it?—two centuries ago?"

"And I don't want it to end." Eduardo takes both of my hands in his.

"Me neither," I say, finally discarding my habit of first denying what I truly feel.

"Let's start with, where are you planning to live?"

"Good question. I don't know."

After a long pause, Eduardo says, "Jenny, I am asking you to stay on here with me and let us see where this takes us."

There's nothing I want more than to share my life with Eduardo for as long as it works for both of us. But I momentarily relapse into an evasive reply.

"We've only known each other for a matter of days," I say.

"I knew Isabella for almost a year before we became involved. A lot of good that did us. We can only find out if our feelings for each other go deeper if we share our lives together. I'm not doing this just to help you. This is really important for me. Please say yes."

"Yes," I say, tears brimming up, "Yes. I would love to share our lives for as long as we both want this. I know this seems premature, but I love you in a way I've never loved anyone before." I get up and bend down to kiss him lingeringly on the lips.

I break the spell by returning to my chair and say, "But—"

"I don't want your 'buts,'" Eduardo interjects.

"But first I have to find a decent job."

"Funny you mention that," he grins. "I was going to ask you what kind of job you are now thinking of applying for."

"All I know is that it cannot be another part-time, temporary, let's-get-by kind of job. It has to be worth doing, and it has to pay me a living wage."

"And what do you consider a living wage?"

"A minimum of $50,000 a year, with benefits, and with the prospect of increases based on performance."

Eduardo clasps his hands together in delight. "Almost exactly what I had in mind."

"What do you mean, you had in mind?"

"I want to make you a job offer."

"*What?*" Now I really feel that I'm dreaming.

"I want you to work for the Coalition as a researcher."

Just as I'm opening my mouth to reject this as a disguised act of charity, Eduardo continues: "I've been in desperate need of an assistant who can take the initiative without much oversight and pursue a project to a conclusion. You fit the job description perfectly."

"Well, thank you for the compliment."

"You deserve it. Nothing is going to change the treatment of immigrants until we have enough votes to compel the government to change the present laws. I want to find ways of doing that while exposing the false information put out by the likes of Dan Granger. I guess I'm wanting a combination of researcher and campaigner. Are you interested?"

"It certainly sounds like a job that would combine earning a living with following the inclinations of my head—and my heart."

"Great."

"What exactly would it pay?"

"Thanks to you and the check you solicited on our behalf, I can meet all your criteria and a little more. So, $55,000 a year, health benefits, and a performance review after a year. What do you say?"

My head is spinning. Still, I have the clarity of mind to say, "I don't think it would be healthy for us to spend all our time together, at the office and at home. Too symbiotic, don't you think?"

"That won't be a problem. Your job will be out in the field. You'll need to report back to the office one half day a week. Otherwise you'll either be out talking to people and searching out information, or home accessing data on the computer."

"Sounds a lot more interesting and fun than watching videos of workers in pain or faking disabilities."

"Then you accept my offer?"

"You bet I do. Thank you so much, Eduardo."

"I suggest you start next Monday. I'm planning to take the rest of the week off. That will barely give us enough time to get out of the bedroom." He grins at me.

"We won't have to leave at all if we order in our meals," I say.

"Perfect," he says. "Let's start now."

*

Hours later I wake up naked in bed. The Business News section of the *LA Times* is lying crumpled at the foot of the bed. I reach out to throw it to the floor, then catch sight of the headline at the top of the front page:

BLUERIM MAKES $80 MILLION IN 1ˢᵀ QUARTER

My eye wanders to the bottom half of the page. In a single column in smaller type I see:

COALITION FOR IMMIGRANT RIGHTS TO RECEIVE

$1 MILLION FROM ANONYMOUS DONOR

MIGUEL

Ignacio Allende 103

68120 Oaxaca,

Oax., Mexico

November 3

Dear Mamá and Papá,

How I miss you. How I miss West Covina. I was such an idiot to take on those officers from ICE. Now it's too late. I'm stuck here where I cannot even speak the language. Yes, I know I will eventually learn it. But it's all so bewildering. I feel completely lost. The only member of the family here who knows even a very small amount of English is my twelve-year-old cousin, Teresa. So there's no one I can talk to.

My grandparents have been great, welcoming me into their family. They made a small space in Uncle Roberto's bedroom for me to sleep in. But the house is so small and so many relatives live in it, or come to spend the day there. I feel terribly selfish wanting a room of my own. But this communal living that they all enjoy leaves me desperate for my own space. All I can do is take myself off for long walks, which help a little.

Have you seen Adela yet? Of course, she must have told you how I got arrested. Mamá, I know you don't much like Adela. But please remember she will be as devastated as we all are at what's happened. Please be kind to her and tell her I miss her so much. I don't have her address, so I can't write to her. Could you ask her to write to me and include her address? On second thought, maybe you shouldn't do that. I don't want to hold on to her when we can no longer see each other. She should be free to find someone else. Just writing that makes me sick to my stomach.

Tomorrow Grandpa is taking me with him to the fields. How strange it will feel after spending my whole life in the city. I guess it will toughen me up physically. But digging and hoeing and raking is not what I want to be spending my life doing. I was looking forward to working on the computer controls of modern cars. I don't think I'm the outdoors type. But that's all I can do for now to earn some money.

Why is the United States so obsessed with us Mexican immigrants? We never asked them for help getting by. We paid our taxes. I worked my butt off at Cal Fowl. What have I done to them to make them so afraid of me? How can they go on splitting up families like ours?

I know. I'm asking the wrong people. I wish I could ask the President in person.

I feel such an anomaly. Like an old man at a rave party. This household feels like one ongoing party. It's a marvel. And yet for me it's incomprehensible. I want my privacy back. I want to be able to choose what I do with my time. There are moments when I want to shout at everyone: Go away! Then I feel awful.

I'm so lost. I miss you two so much. I miss my friends, and college, and Adela, and just sitting up in bed with my laptop open in my own room.

But what's the use?

Your loving, lost son,

Miguel

THE END

AUTHOR BIOGRAPHY

Brian Finney is a Professor Emeritus of Literature at California State University, Long Beach. Educated in England, he obtained a BA from the University of Reading and a PhD from the University of London. After serving three years as an officer in the Royal Air Force, he spent five years in industry as an internal management consultant and production control manager. Between 1964 and 1987 he taught and arranged extramural courses for the University of London. Since immigrating to the US in 1987 he has taught at the University of California, Riverside, University of Southern California, UCLA, and California State University, Long Beach.

He has written eight books, including a prizewinning biography of Christopher Isherwood and *Terrorized*, a nonfiction book about the effects of the war on terror on American culture and society (available on Kindle).

He is married and lives in Venice, California.

www.ingramcontent.com/pod-product-compliance
Lightning Source LLC
Chambersburg PA
CBHW070449120726
47910CB00003B/989